HOLOCAUST

HEARTS

BJ Swann + Elizabeth Bedlam

Cover by: Elizabeth Bedlam

Typesetting by: **ELIZABETH BEDLAM**

Punk AF Logos designed by Caelan Stokker mans Arts

Published by: **PUNK AF PUBLSHING** + **BEDLAM ! TYPEHOUSE**

Copyright 2021 by: BJ Swann + Elizabeth Bellam

BEDLAM ! TYPEHOUSE

bedlam ! typehouse

Bedlam ! Typehouse
Michigan, USA
Instagram: @elizabeth.bedlam
Email: elizabethbedlam@gmail.com
Website: elizabethbedlam.com

Punk AF Publishing
The Upside Down
Email: bjswann@aeonofchaos.com
Website: www.aeonofchaos.com

Contents

1

Drowning in Viscera

SILFER HURRIED DOWN the street, head down, trying not to knock into anyone. The surrounding buildings were draped in human souls, all of them flayed and vivisected. Their excavated organs bloomed like awful flowers; their nerve fibers stretched across the crumbling red hell-bricks like vines.

The souls screamed in agony as Stygian winds blew across their innards. The cries were carried from their mouths by grimy brass tubes that snaked up the walls and jutted from the tops of the buildings like pipes from a church organ. The metal channels amplified and distorted the screams, creating an endless, tuneless cacophony some people called "The Music of Hell."

Some devils loved the sound; they could listen to it all day long. Silfer found it fucking annoying. Which was why he had his headphones on, his iPod cranked to full volume (yes, they have iPods in Hell. Steve Jobs makes them all in a sweatshop). Silfer was listening to one of his favorite bands, Excruciate Rex. He always thought the only really good thing about Hell was the music scene. All the best musicians were there.

Excruciate Rex was a supergroup that included underground sensations like Dead, Bianca Butthole, Keith Moon, and Nero (the Roman Emperor, not the British techno trio). If Silfer had to describe their music to a mortal, he'd say it was like black metal punk crossed with opera and produced by John Zorn. But that would only be a vague approximation of the band's true strangeness.

Excruciate Rex was so weird they weren't even that popular. Most demons listened to stuff by souls like Janis Joplin, Mama Cass or Jimi Hendrix. Silfer couldn't stand that mainstream shit. All those people had sold out since they'd landed in Hell. Hendrix didn't even play his own guitar when he sang these days. He made Prince do it.

Silfer stopped at a street corner and went to activate the crossing lights, which were triggered not by a mechanical button, but by a set of exposed testicles belonging to a screaming human soul attached to the street pole by hooks and chains. He yelped as Silfer tapped his nuts, but the sound was mostly lost amidst the ear-shattering screams of the city.

Silfer waited at the curb as cars flashed past, dragging bound corpses behind them. The lights of the intersection flashed red, and a giant stretch Humvee pulled up beside the curb. A group of rich, young douchebag devils were partying in the back, poking their heads through the human skin sunroof as they listened to the latest shitty collaboration between 2Pac and Biggie Smalls. The young devils screamed and laughed, shouting something incoherent. Silfer ignored them and crossed the road, sighing in irritation as he got to the other side.

Ahead was the Road of Excoriated Souls, which was a pretentious name for a street if ever there was one. Most devils just called it "Chode Road" for short. The pavement was created from skinned human souls, the majority of which were arranged with their asses in the air, so that their perineum, butthole, and the tattered remains of their genitals were exposed to the city's daily grind.

The idea must've seemed cool to someone at some point. But the city's planning council clearly hadn't thought it through very well. As it turned out, walking on a bunch of flayed people's butts was really irritating. An endless road of undulating, blood-slick asses made traffic slow, and walking even slower.

Silfer had to stop and add spikes on his shoes, like the sort people use for walking on black ice. He set off across the gruesome pavement, doing his best not to fall as the bodies wiggled beneath him.

Silfer sighed. A lot of devils were proud of Hell, but he wasn't. The place was just so...trite. At the end of the day, all this endless visceral depravity was grindingly boring. Only a true sadist could enjoy it day in, day out without growing numb. Silfer was as mean as the next demon, but he wasn't exceptionally cruel. He'd been bored with the whole thing for as long as he could remember.

Even a lot of mortals found it boring. He'd seen their reactions when he'd worked briefly as an orientation guide for the recently damned. Sure, many people freaked out, started crying and screaming, covering their eyes, calling on God, Buddha, Muhammad, whatever. But some of them *didn't* flip out. They were the ones who'd lived really fucked-up lives on earth – cartel sicarios, concentration camp inmates, people who'd served time in South African prisons. When people that jaded saw what lay before them, some smiled and laughed. Others – the ones who'd managed to keep a smidgen of sensitivity through the horrors they'd endured on earth – just looked around sadly. "This is it?" they'd say. "*This* is the afterlife? I thought it would be more, you know, transcendental. More ineffable, more magical..."

"No, sorry, this is it," Silfer would reply.

Some might shrug and take it in stride; others would be really affronted.

"Is this a joke?" they'd ask. "This is like a

bad South Park episode!"

"Sorry," Silfer would say again, shrugging. "But this is it. This is Hell."

And really, what did they expect? Why should the afterlife be any less banal than life itself? Transcendental things weren't real. They only existed in the minds of poets – or perhaps in the fathomless, symbiotic space between the hearts of two people in love. Otherwise it was all a humdrum shitshow. Heaven, Hell, Earth, whatever. On every plane of existence you still had to tie your shoelaces and do your taxes. There was no escape from banality, only in dreams.

What bothered Silfer though was that things didn't have to be as stupid as they were. That was the fault of the people in charge. In Hell, it was the fault of the Infernal Engineers. They were the ones who designed the torments for the damned. They were like writers, movie directors, and torturers all rolled into one. They were supposed to be the most brilliant creative minds Hell had to offer, but that was bullshit. For centuries the engineers had been appointed on the basis of nepotism and cronyism.

As on earth, it's not what you know, it's who you blow. You could only be an engineer if you went to the right private school or had the right uncle. Which probably explained why the engineers themselves were clearly some of the most vacuous, pedestrian content creators in the cosmos. The current engineers hadn't had an original idea since Christ walked on water. They simply plagiarized writers from Earth, then sought to justify it with all sorts of pretentious metatextual bullocks, claiming it was the "ultimate torture" to let humanity design its personal Hell through its own art and literature. But Silfer knew the truth – the engineers were just rip-off artists, pure and simple. For centuries the creators of Hell had ripped off the Greeks and Romans. Making people push rocks up hillsides over and over. Tying them to the sides of mountains so vultures could eat their guts. Lashing them to flaming wheels. When that got old, they began ripping off Dante. For ages and ages everything was Dante *this,* Dante *that*. Did you hear what Dante said? Soon Hell had its own oceans of shit for the flatterers to float in, fiery deserts for the wrathful, whipping winds for horny people to get buffeted by.

Silfer's shittiest job – literally – had been torturing the flatterers. Mostly he'd had to hang out beside a shit pool, shoving them back in with a stick if they tried to get out. Sometimes one would escape onto the bank and have to be recaptured. Ever try to wrestle with a desperate soul covered in sticky black shit? It's as bad as it sounds. Silfer quit after only two days.

The engineers loved Dante so much they'd even had Hell remodeled with nine fucking layers! Talk about a lack of originality. The engineers were worse than Hollywood. These days they'd moved away from the literary classics, and had taken to mostly ripping off extreme horror authors like Clive Barker and Wrath James White. A welcome change of pace, yet still too derivative for Silfer's liking. He felt sure he'd be able to come up with better stuff if *he* were an engineer.

Silfer often spent hours dreaming of the torments he'd create. He'd get rid of all this crass body horror stuff. No more using people as traffic lights. No more force-feeding people feces. No more Chode Road. He'd make it more subtle, more cerebral. He'd trap souls in fantasies, forcing them to re-live repeatedly the very worst moments of their lives. And if they tried to escape? They'd end up in a labyrinth without end. From the broken sky above the laughter of their parents would echo like thunder.

Now wouldn't that be something? Sub-tle, sophisticated, soul-destroying – *that* would be a Hell he could be proud of. But of course, Silfer would never get to be an En-gineer; he didn't have the pedigree. Plus, if he really thought about it, he didn't want to be one anyway. He was only drawn towards the occupation because he liked to dream. But his greatest dreams weren't about tor-turing souls. His greatest dreams were only for him. Fantasies so impossible and sweet they made his heart ache. Dreams about things most devils didn't even think about. Dreams that stopped him from going in-sane.

Silfer took the spikes off his shoes as he arrived at his destination, an art deco build-ing marked 333. He made his way through a revolving door made from screaming human souls stretched across a lattice of bone. Why didn't the volume on his iPod go up any louder? Fucking thing must have been faulty. Steve Jobs was shit at process work.

He strode through the lobby, ignoring the security desk and making straight for the elevator. A she-devil in a fitted suit was already waiting. She was pretty, but Silfer knew he'd have nothing in common with her. He never had anything in common with anyone.

Together they rode the lift in silence, she scrolling through her iPhone, he listening to music. The lift was a transparent cube dragged up a shaft by loops of intestines whose owners were impaled on the top floor. Their screams echoed downwards.

Silfer got off the lift first and walked down a dingy corridor. He arrived at his destination, the office of Infernal Employment Services, which was no doubt the most generic fucking name for a job agency in Hell anyone could have possibly come up with.

"Hi," he said, approaching the receptionist, a new devil girl he'd never seen before. "I'm Silfer Incinerator, I've got an appointment with Sunny Badmoon?"

"Oh, hello, Mr. Incinerator." She flashed a friendly smile. "Let me just check your details."

She started typing something on her Apple computer. Her sparkly nails were so long and claw-like it was a miracle she could type at all. She had to splay her fingers out and extend them till they curved slightly upwards. It looked uncomfortable. Was it really worth all the hassle just to have huge fucking fingernails? He didn't get it.

Silfer waited, feeling a familiar nervousness swell up in his guts. "Incinerator" was his legal name, but it wasn't his birth name. He hated his birth name, hence why he'd changed it to something nice and normal like Incinerator (a lot of devil last names came from classic devil occupations – Skinner, Impaler, Violator, Eviscerator, Defiler, etc.). But of course his birth name was in his file on the computer. He could change it, but he could never truly escape it. It followed him around like stigmata, like the scars on his body. He waited for the inevitable moment when the receptionist would see his real name and look at him differently, with eyes of alienation, contempt, mistrust. But she must have just been skim-reading, because she smiled at him politely as she looked up from the screen.

"Sunny's gone," she said. "He quit."

"He did?"

"Yeah, but you're booked in with Karla. Office number three-zero-six. You can go in there now."

Silfer shrugged, thanked her, and headed for the office. He found the door open. A heavyset devil woman sat in a chair in front of computer. She glanced over at him.

"Silfer?" she said.

There was something reserved in her manner, something arrogant and cold, something that said *I've read your file. I've seen your real last name. And I know what you are, you piece of red trash.*

"Yeah," he said.

"Hi, I'm Karla. Please come in."

"Nice to meet you," he said, sitting across from her. She typed something into the keyboard. Her nails were also huge, glittery, and claw-like; she had to splay her fingers and extend them awkwardly in order to type. What was with these women? You'd think if your job was typing all day long, a person would just cut their nails off and save themselves the constant discomfort.

She glanced at the computer, then at him.

"So, I've had a look at your resume," she said. "And honestly, it's not very good. Have you thought about up-skilling?"

Silfer sighed. "Can you get me a job or what?"

"Well, there might be a few things on our books you'd be suitable for. Let me see..." She tapped on the keys. "Oh, okay. There's a job at Screwhide Mill shoving red-hot pokers up people's assholes."

"Nope," said Silfer.

"Okay," she said, scrolling down. "Well, how about this? They need people to sew damned souls into a human centipede. You know, like that movie from Earth. It says the candidate should have no experience performing surgeries at all, to maximize the pain and bloodshed. So you'd be suitable. It's minimum wage, but there will be a lot of hours available, casual rates –"

"Pass," said Silfer.

"Okay," she said, her words holding an

edge of controlled irritation. "It looks like I have one more opening here. It's a sales job, paid on commission, so you might not even make ends meet. But they'll take basically anyone."

"What is it?" he asked.

"Tempting human souls on earth. You'd go up in spectral form. No material incarnation, obviously, that would be against the Hezekiah Pact. But you'd be able to appear to whoever you want, in any shape you desire. The tough part is, you'd have to net about thirty souls a day to make it even remotely worthwhile."

Silfer paused to think. Tempting human beings for a pissy commission sounded like a real grind. But what other choice did he have? Besides, he'd never even been to Earth. "Sure, I'll fucking take it." he said, thinking *who knows? It might be interesting.*

Silfer took a swig of his beer. He figured he was entitled to a celebration for getting a new job. Even if it was a shitty job he'd probably quit in a week. But of course he didn't like to drink alone, so he'd invited Rust.

Rust was ostensibly his best friend. But when Silfer thought about it, maybe Rust wasn't really a friend at all. All he did was talk incessantly, mostly about himself. When he wasn't talking, he sure as shit wasn't listening. You could tell he was inside his own head, mentally rehearsing what he was going to say next, like an actor waiting to go on stage. Why did he even bother having conversations with people at all? He could just cut out all the bother and deliver monologues in front of a mirror.

"...And then Andre the Giant gave him a triple suplex, ripped out his spine, and shoved it up his ass!"

Rust was talking about professional wrestling again, even though Silfer had told him many times he wasn't interested in it. It was more exciting than wrestling on Earth, because of the constant murder and dismemberment, but Silfer still thought it was silly. He took a drag of his cigarette, then stubbed it out on the ashtray's eye. The ashtray was a human head. It groaned and wept. Silfer ignored it. Rust kept talking about wrestling. Then he recited a bunch of comedy routines almost verbatim, ruining the timing, making sure Silfer would never bother actually watching the original material. Silfer couldn't get a word in edgewise. He glanced off at the stage, where Roy Orbison was singing "Only the Lonely." His trademark dark glasses covered the empty sockets of his eyes.

Fuck, this song is depressing, thought Silfer. He felt a melancholy rose bloom in his heart, heavy, wet, and bittersweet. He took another drink.

"Then Harpo takes the scissors, and cuts his nuts off!"

Rust was now ruining the plot to the new Marx Brothers film, which basically featured the Marx Brothers torturing the Warner Brothers. Apparently it was hilarious. Without taking a breath, Rust ran on talking about the labyrinthine politics that dominated the office he worked at. Silfer knew all the details, all the personalities intimately.

"So, do you think I should take Terri into the stationary closet and show her my cock?"

"I don't know, Rust. I think that might backfire."

"Okay. But what about my supervisor, Stu? Should I tell him I've got ass cancer? It might stop him hassling me about all these deadlines."

"That's probably not the best idea. What if everyone starts sending you flowers and get-well cards? Besides, how are you going to explain it when you're not sick at all?"

"Good point. But what about that douche Greg? He's totally trying to undermine me. I think I should spread a rumor he sniffs the girls' seats while they're on lunch break."

Silfer shrugged. "Sure, why not?"

Rust took out his phone and started scrolling through social media apps. Maybe he'd received a message; maybe it was just a compulsion he had to fulfill. Either way, the table was quiet for the first time in almost two hours. With Rust's voice finally gone, there was only the chatter of the bar, the screaming of the ashtrays, and the sound of the Big O singing "In Dreams."

This was Silfer's chance to talk, get some things off his chest. But what could he say?

Rust wouldn't understand. Maybe no one would. The things he needed to talk about, people just didn't want to hear. He took a swig of his beer.

"Sometimes I feel terribly lonely," he began. "Like no one could possibly understand me. Like I'm on a different wavelength or something. No one can know the ecstasy, the agony I feel when I'm alone in my head. I think I've got the soul of an artist. Sometimes I just want to burn up in flames and leave only ashes. Or just fade away. I'm not meant for this world. I can't stand the banality. It's like sandpaper on my soul every day. I can't relate to anyone. I sure as shit can't relate to you. All you do is talk bullshit. You're so fucking boring. It's like you're dead inside. Do you even have a soul, or did someone hollow you out and fill you up with beige? Did you ever even *dream*? There's no connection between us. I might as well be talking to the ashtray. Sometimes I dream of strange things, of finding something, someone, far away from here..."

"Huh? What was that, buddy?" asked Rust as he scrolled through Twitter, which, contrary to popular belief on Earth, had actually been invented in Hell.

"You didn't hear anything I just said, did you?"

"Sure, man, totally. Hold on, I've gotta take a leak."

Still staring at his phone, Rust rose and stumbled towards the bathroom, already drunk. He'd probably piss all over the floor, totally missing all the human head toilet bowls. Which would certainly be a relief for the toilet bowls, if not for the other human heads with long frizzy hair, impaled on sticks, who'd be used to mop up the mess.

Silfer sighed to himself for the umpteenth time that day. "Hey," said the ashtray. "I hear you, man. You know, I can totally relate. I've got it pretty bad too."

"Shut the fuck up," said Silfer.

He put his cigarette out on the ashtray's tongue and left the bar.

"Spare some change?" begged Hitler. Silfer pushed the old hobo aside and stepped into the lobby of the apartment building. The place was grimy and covered with graffiti. Raised voices and blaring music seeped through the doors and echoed down the stairwell. Shards of glass crunched as Silfer climbed the stairs to the top level. On the landing, a young she-devil was passed out with a needle jutting from her arm. A man crouched over her, licking her, her pretty face slack and covered in spittle.

Silfer stepped over them both and made his way to the end of the hall. He rapped on a door covered in neon-pink graffiti. It flew open, revealing three beautiful succubi, one purple, one red, one blue. Kiki, CeeCee, and DeeDee were their names. They claimed to be sisters, but whether that was true was anyone's guess.

"Silfer!" said Kiki. "Where have you been?"

"Looking for work," he said as they dragged him inside. "But I finally got a job."

"What job?" Asked DeeDee, pulling off his coat. Made from lost souls, the coat groaned as it was stripped from his shoulders and tossed on the floor.

"Tempting souls on earth."

"Oh!" said CeeCee. "We used to do that! We made a killing. So many virgin males, ha-ha."

"Why am I not surprised?" said Silfer. The sisters were insatiable. Silfer was one of their many casual lovers. For a while he'd been addicted to their charms, but lately he'd been avoiding them. They could be so utterly demanding. All they ever thought about was sex. They were like libidos on legs. Still, tonight he wanted them. The alcohol had failed to put him in an altered state of mind. He craved the oblivion of orgasm, the fleeting transcendence of fucking.

As they tore off the last of his clothes, he noticed a naked human captive in the corner of the room, chained and terrified.

"Don't get him involved," said Silfer. "I didn't like that last time."

"Sure, Sil!" Said Kiki. "No problem."

Like an angry mob the sisters dragged him to the bed and threw him down. Next thing he knew Kiki was on top of him, kissing him. Her serpentine tongue swirled with his. Someone was tonguing his prick. Was it CeeCee or DeeDee? He glanced down and saw it was both of them together, swapping the shaft between their mouths and fervently licking his balls.

The fellatio didn't last very long. A second later DeeDee was taking him inside. Kiki mounted his face, fucking his mouth with her cunt. He stuck out his tongue and did his best to lick. She rocked back and forth, her thighs squeezing his head. Her pubes above his eyes blocked out the world; her rising moans blocked out the noise of the streets.

Someone, it must have been CeeCee (he sure hoped it wasn't the guy in the corner) grabbed his right hand and licked it all over. He could tell it really was CeeCee as soon as she pushed his fist into her cunt.

Silfer took his free hand and grabbed Kiki's ass. He tried to switch off his consciousness, detach from his stupid whirling thoughts about his shitty career, his so-called friends, his vast and unsatisfied longings. He focused on the velvet strength of DeeDee's cunt, the juices in his mouth, the clit on his tongue.

Silfer's thoughts slipped away. His consciousness shrank to a wordless awareness of nothing but the flickering messages of pleasure flashing from his prick. DeeDee rode him, her hot cunt gripping and sliding, sparking brighter flashes of ecstasy with each undulating movement. Steadily the space between each instant of bliss became shorter and shorter, till the pauses were elided with overlapping pleasure, a searing concentration of pleasure that enveloped his flesh like an inferno. Flickering blackness covered his eyes, wherein stars seemed to flash into being and then suddenly die, as though he were witnessing a spectacle of cosmic creation and subsequent genocide.

Still too busy eating cunt to speak, he tapped on DeeDee's thigh to let her know he'd cum. She took the hint and rode him slowly, gently squeezing out the last of his climax. But it wasn't over. The succubus sisters were far from being satisfied...

Later he lay on the bed, smoking, while the three sisters licked at each other, spattered with their fluids and his. As often he felt strangely empty. The ecstasy was always fleeting. Was there something wrong with him? Maybe he was just one of those demons who could never be satisfied.

In many ways Silfer was a prosperous devil. He knew he should be happy. He'd escaped the shithole he'd been born into. He was thrifty, so even though he'd worked only dead-end jobs for the past several years, he still had a healthy savings account. Plus, he got to have wild sex with the succubus sisters pretty much whenever he wanted. Countless mortals had literally given their souls for such an experience. So why wasn't it enough from him? Why couldn't it match his incandescent dreams? If he was more like Rust, he'd be on cloud nine right now.

Silfer got up and went to the bathroom. When he got back, the sisters had their captive on the bed, spread-eagle. DeeDee was sitting on his face. Spider-like legs extended from her labia, wrapping around his head. Vaginal teeth ripped the skin from his skull and devoured it. Slowly his entire face – hair, lips, nose, eyelids, and scalp – were dragged into her ravenous gash. Silfer was glad she'd never tried that trick with him. The captive twitched, unable to scream. His lidless eyes rolled back, spinning, darting, as though seeking to escape their own sockets.

"You want to join in?" asked DeeDee, her face brimming with lust.

"Nah," said Silfer. "I've got to get an early start on this new job."

"Aw," said the sisters, pouting simultaneously. "Come back soon!"

"I will," he said, not sure if he was lying
or not.

2

Infinite Misery

MARA WAS AWAKE before her alarm
went off, but the heaviness in her chest kept
her from rising.

Another day.

She honestly didn't think she could bear
it, knowing what it had in store for her. The
same as the day before, and the day before
that, and the day before that.

She lay beneath her quilt, wondering
how her life had become this endless cy-
cle of work and home with few variations
thrown in. Maybe she'd stop at the grocery store on the corner. Perhaps she'd go
out with Kathy from work and have a drink.
Maybe just pick up takeout from the same
old restaurant. They knew her by name

now. Perhaps she'd take the long way home through the park, weather permitting. None of it really mattered. All days ended the same - her alone in her apartment, wondering why she was still there. Killing time until she was tired enough to go to sleep.

The endless stream of thoughts made her angry. Mara wasn't sure why she didn't do something about it. She could switch apartments, change jobs, move to another city. Go north where it was cold, or south where it was hot. But she stayed here in this concrete hell, clinging to the edge of a polluted river. Maybe because it was safe, familiar. Probably because she was afraid.

Mara wanted to think she was brave, but knew she was a coward. She always did everything everyone expected her to do. She'd finished school a year early. Gone to university. Got a job working in the archive department at the museum, every day cleaning paper frail from age, vacuuming dust from leather editions of antique texts. Sitting for endless hours running a cotton swab slowly, evenly down a page, removing centuries of grime.

Hadn't that been the appeal in the first

place? The idea of sitting in a dim room with hundreds of silent old books, some so valuable no one would ever see or touch them but for a few select hands? She'd thought it a worthy vocation. At first it had been. Yet nearly a decade later, her passion had become just a job, no different from that of a fry cook or a banker. A place she went each day to earn money to pay her rent or buy her food. The beauty of ancient pages had been reduced to a paycheck. This depressed her more than anything.

The alarm repeated a third time.

"God, shut up."

She rolled over, dismissed the alarm, and forced herself up. She sat on the edge of the bed, glaring at the sun leaking through the cracks of her heavy curtains. She knew it would be another hot day, and it wasn't even eight.

Mara could never decide if she hated Mondays or looked forward to them. She had the same problem with Fridays. Endless free time and she never knew what to do with herself; scheduled office hours, she felt trapped and bored.

In the kitchen she clicked on the radio.

It was old and barely picked up local stations. She listened to the news a moment, decided she hated everything, and turned the dial, stopping on the first loud angry noise she came to. Tried and true west coast thrash. Simple, easy to listen to, all about death and war and hate. The last thing she wanted to hear about was love and kindness and hugs.

"Before you see the light, you must die..."

Mara nodded along. *Yeah, that sounds pretty fucking good right now.*

She dug through her cabinet and pulled out a bag of coffee, realized it was empty, and tossed it in the trash. Now she'd have to stop and buy more. Today Mara decided she hated Mondays.

Mara stepped onto the sidewalk and let her eyes adjust to the sun. She sighed, looking at the ever-changing neighborhood surrounding her humble apartment building. The city was losing the lovely melancholy Mara had cherished. The noises, the traffic, the gunfire had lost their aggression.

Everything was just... different. Gang graffiti was being replaced with upbeat murals of flying doves and sunshine.

Not to mention now that housing had become dirt cheap, twenty-year-old blonde couples were swooping in to buy up all the dilapidated Tudors and Victorians, hoping to turn them into Instagram-worthy houses. This meant white on gray on white with decorating styles called "Boho-chic" or "Scandi farmhouse industrial." Puke! Mara preferred her style – "Urban Graveyard." A mix of thrift store buys, trash found on the street, and vintage pieces salvaged from derelict lunatic asylums. Her coffee table had once been the headstone of a woman named Emma Von Bergen who'd died in 1912. She'd found it in an unkempt yard in Westland. Perfect! No need for coasters.

Walking down the sidewalk towards work, Mara wanted to rip her eyes out as she saw that her new neighbors, Todd and Cara, had chopped down a hundred-year-old oak tree and planted a Bradford Pear in its place. It would be dead from fire blight in a year! Mara couldn't stand the new couple. They'd invited her in last week to see their renovations. Cara had painted all the original woodwork white to make the space feel "light and bright!" They'd put carpeting over hardwood floors. Todd had knocked down all the walls to create an open floor plan. Mara couldn't decide which offense was the worst; she went with all of them.

Jesus Christ, I've got to get out of this city, Mara thought, rushing past the half-dead sapling and turning the corner. The sidewalks were already crowded with wealthy young urban couples shopping in the new hip stores that sold overpriced healing crystals and artisan goat cheese.

On the corner, a yoga studio had opened last fall. All the women were terribly slender and wore pants that cost more than her rent. Mara remembered when that yoga studio had been a porn studio. The city had shut it down after they'd discovered the directors weren't checking to make sure their performers were of age.

Mara pushed into the tiny coffee shop, nearly colliding with the hoard of young mothers pushing overly lavish strollers on their way to the children's museum. Inside, Mara ordered a black coffee that cost too much.

"What about some flavoring? We also do latte art now. It's so beautiful!"

Every fucking time, Mara thought. She was in this place at least four days a week, and still they hassled her to fancify her beverage.

"No, black. Just plain old black," she insisted to the eighteen-year-old girl behind the counter, who didn't seem to understand the concept of coffee that wasn't slathered in weird cinnamon or salted caramel bullshit.

The girl shrugged. *Whatever, lady*, her eyes plainly said. Mara thought twice about it, but put her change in the tip jar anyway. Being a coffee slave probably didn't pay shit.

She pulled her sunglasses on. Threading her way down the sidewalk among the early morning shoppers, urban professionals, and mobs of school children heading to one place or the other, she couldn't help but wonder, *where had all the crazy people gone*?

Mara missed them wandering the streets. Sometimes they'd come up to you, start talking about some vision they'd had of the afterlife.

"No shit?" Mara had said, when a ragged woman, who'd been kicked out of the Eloise Asylum back in the early 1980s, had started going on about her vision of the other side.

"I was dead for three minutes. I saw the Devil coming to collect my soul for killin' my husband! But them doctors restarted my heart. It was a close call. This world is all an illusion! Hell is waiting for us. The end is near! Repent sinner!" She screamed, shaking a fist at Mara and anyone else who passed by.

"Sure. Yeah. Wicked." Mara said, offering the woman a cigarette and a cup of coffee.

That was back then. Today, if you smoked, people looked at you like you had two heads. Mara had been lectured on multiple occasions by kids half her age for smoking while walking down the street or sitting outside a cafe.

"Those won't just kill you, you know. You're putting all of us at risk," a ninety-pound baby barely out of a training bra had once remarked, glaring at Mara. The baby's friends nodded and rolled their eyes, while Mara took an even deeper hit off her cigarette and exhaled in their general direction.

"I hope you die of cancer!" they cursed as they walked away, vape clouds trailing behind them.

Mara turned right and crossed the wide grass courtyard. She pulled her museum ID out, flashed it at the elderly ticket taker, and passed by the line already forming. It was early, but people were milling around waiting to get into the Schiele exhibit that had opened Friday. Paintings of awkward nudes. Mostly teenage prostitutes, or Schiele himself, fucking teenage prostitutes. Long-dead derelict women and their vaginas.

The room was closed off and had signs warning guests of the erotic nature of his paintings. Mara shook her head. Everything needed a warning these days. It was a fucking art museum. What had happened to the idea that art was supposed to be dangerous and confrontational? Mara pushed between a group of middle schoolers waiting to get into the exhibit. She took a left and descended the stairs into the museum's library and archives department.

It was a drastic change from the airy museum overhead. Silent, cold, beige. A labyrinth of metal shelves and endless texts. This morning it was mostly empty, save for art history majors and researchers from the nearby university. No one looked up as she passed. She used her card to let herself into the back rooms for technicians and conservators.

She heard Kathy before she saw her. That laugh of hers, like a braying donkey in heat. Mara kept her head down and tried to pass the small break room unnoticed.

"Mara!" Kathy yelled, perverting the sacred silence of the library. "I tried calling you. Mara!"

Mara pretended she didn't hear and kept walking. Kathy followed, quick for such a thick woman.

"You didn't call me back!" she squawked.

Mara paused just inside her office. Kathy was her boss. Outside of work she could avoid her if she wanted; inside she had no choice but to force a smile and make soul-killing small talk.

"Did you call? Sorry. My phone must

have been turned off. I had no idea." Mara took a sip of coffee and looked away from Kathy's intense eye contact. "What's all this?" she asked, noticing a weathered crate beside her desk.

"Oh, that's one of the things I wanted to show you." Kathy ushered Mara into the room, giving her no choice but to go with her. "I told you these would be coming. Don't you remember?"

Mara thought about it. Kathy said so many things. It was hard to keep track. She just nodded anyway, glancing at the faded red stamp on top of the crate reading "Kutna Hora."

"Where the hell is that?" She asked.

Kathy looked clueless. Mara raised the lid and looked down at a grim pile of discolored, crumbling leather books tossed carelessly inside.

"Wow, it smells. What is that? Who owned these?" she asked, taking a step back and setting her coffee down on the table.

"Well, that's the mystery, isn't? The museum bought all these at a closed auction. Apparently most of them were found under the floor during the renovations of the

Sedlec Ossuary. The church was selling them, hoping to raise the funds to repair the roof. They look old, don't they? What do you think?"

Kathy may have been head of the department, but Mara figured that was probably just because she was married to the museum director. In fact, Mara had never seen Kathy do anything other than talk, look over people's shoulders, gossip, and rearrange exhibits after they'd already been set up.

"I'll have to look at them, Kathy. But judging by the leather, and the smell, I'd say they were under that floor for a while."

Kathy stood, waiting for Mara to take a book out. Watching like an impatient child.

"I have to wash my hands. I need to set up my table. It's going to be awhile, Kathy. I'll let you know."

Mara turned away and walked to the sink. Kathy looked somewhat upset, as if she were being left out. None of the technicians would ever let her watch.

When Mara offered nothing else, Kathy dragged herself towards the door.

"Well, that's fine then, uh, let me know what you find out. Maybe sooner rather than later."

Mara didn't bother responding. Any hint, a single word, could draw Kathy back in, and Mara would never get rid of her. Kathy took a last look and left. Mara could finally breathe. She closed the door before Kathy could think of an excuse to come back. God, it took so long just to start the day. She didn't understand why Kathy couldn't just leave her a note, or just say what she had to say and leave. This was a job, not a social gathering. Mara sighed, she just had to forget it. If she spent all her time trying to figure out people like Kathy, she'd end up under the desk eating her own nail clippings. Or even worse, she'd end up like Kathy. Constantly talking, but saying nothing. That made Mara feel a little better. At least she wasn't like Kathy. *That* was something.

She clicked on her light table, then turned to the crate, removing the lid completely and looking inside. She gasped at the smell, now wafting out stronger than ever. Mara had come across plenty of musty books. Usually it was the binding glue that gave them that dusty attic stench. But this

was different. The box was overpowering-
ly cloying to a degree that made Mara feel
sick. She sat on her stool and inhaled her
deep bitter coffee, trying to remove the sickly sweet stench from her nose. A candied rot
was the only way she could describe it.

After a moment, she drew a shallow
breath through her mouth and took out the
top book. The leather was flaking and torn
at the bottom.

"What were they thinking?"

She carefully set the stout volume down
on the support in the middle of her desk.
With skilled hands she opened the book,
careful not to strain the spine. The pages were worn, half eaten away, some water damaged along the bottom. It was impossible to read the text. Damp had washed
much of the ink away over the centuries.

Centuries.

She was sure the books must be five to
six hundred years old. How long had they
been under that floor?

"Fuck, what a waste."

This volume couldn't be helped. It had
too much damage. The leather was flecked
with white mildew. Its deterioration had al-

ready begun long ago.

Setting it aside, Mara spent the rest of the morning going through the stack one by one. A few of the volumes were in better shape than others, but not by much. From what she could tell they were Christian texts. The few illuminations were simple. Faded greens or blues, snaking vines. The style varied from book to book. Some looked half finished. A random collection perhaps, grabbed in haste from a scriptorium. Many books had been hidden like that by monks in fear of being raided by Vikings or the like. Setting the fifth book aside, she now knew only three could be salvaged. The other two couldn't be helped.

Mara stood and stretched, thankful the morning had gone fairly quickly. The smell had somewhat dissipated thanks to the amazing air filtration each of the rooms provided, more for the benefit of the books than that of the employees. Mara went to move the crate into the hall so the janitors could take it away.

"What the..."

She paused above the open crate, noticing a slender leather volume half-hidden amongst the packing material at the bottom. She'd almost missed it. She sat the crate back down and took out the document. It wasn't like the others, more like a leather folder than a book. Curious.

On the soft support, she slowly spread the cracked book skin open. Inside was a stack of wide, tawny, stained pages carelessly folded into quarters. She'd never seen anything like it. They weren't bound in any way, just a pile of loose documents. She looked up at the clock; it was almost lunch. For the first time in a long time, she thought about skipping her break. This was more interesting.

She took out the first page, set it flat beside the book support, and tenderly unfolded a large sheet six times the width and length of an average book. She'd never seen such large pages. At the top was a gilded letter, heavily illustrated, licked by sharp carmine flames. The text below curled from one end of the paper to the other, neatly written with a skilled, steady hand. These pages were not like the other volumes in the crate. Mara instantly knew these were something else completely.

She studied the lettering and quickly concluded it was a mix of at least five old tongues. A few she couldn't even identify.

"Fuck me, what is this?" she muttered.

Mara ran a finger along the edge of the page. It was ragged, as if torn from a greater collection. Spots of black staining, soot maybe, dotted the frayed outer corners.

Forgetting the time, she unfolded the rest of the elaborately illuminated pages and laid them side by side across the light table. Ten in all. All with the same ragged, blackened borders. They'd been ripped from somewhere else, then folded and stored under that floor.

When she came to the last page she sat back, taking in the intricate "H" detailed with gold and black, wrapped with red dragons. She knew there must be an order to the pages. Once they were fully translated, they would surely make more sense. She could understand grains of fractured Hebrew and Greek amongst the mixture of ancient tongues she couldn't place.

And he says...so the time & half a time are 1,260 years...one-half and three years...

Judgment...hour of transition...curso-ry days...inhabit beasts being put forth... the 1,260 prophetic days...the red drag-on crouches...downfall...devastation and destruction...a woman garbed...sun...the remnant...so it's written...end of...

"Jesus Christ, what? End of what?"

Mara leaned closer, squinting, trying to figure out the rest. It read like a prophe-cy of sorts, and not a pleasant one. She gen-tly picked at a flake of black smudged over the last words, hoping to loosen it. The lon-ger she looked, the deeper the inks seemed to become. Undulating, almost flickering in the faint light of the room.

Mara blinked her eyes. They felt sud-denly dry, as if someone had blown smoke in them. The more she read, the richer, the warmer the text became. Bewitching her, inviting her to come closer still, to see, to read. Somewhere in the back of her mind, she knew she shouldn't. A whisper told her not to, but she ignored it. For a second she thought she saw the words clearly, as if they made sense. Like the book was translating them for her.

Her door flew open, knocking into the wall.

"Mara! You're still here? It's past one. Come have lunch with me!" Kathy said.

It took Mara a moment to come back to Earth. Her pulse thundered in her ears. She struggled to focus on her boss in the doorway. What had she just been reading? What were these pages?

"Mara, whatever is the matter? You look pale."

Mara forced herself to look away from the brilliant sheets laid out across her table.

"Do you think we could have Chris look at these?" she asked. "I only know half of what it says. I don't even recognize some of these languages."

She looked from Kathy back to the pages. Kathy seemed puzzled and offered no help. It was lunch, Kathy never worked through lunch.

"Forget it," said Mara. "Maybe I should eat something."

Her blood sugar was probably low. She needed a cigarette. She hadn't been sleeping enough lately. She got tense over nothing when she was tired and hungry.

Mara left the pages on the desk and turned off the lights, locking the door behind her as she left.

Mara waited all afternoon, staring at the pages, trying to read them, wondering what was taking Chris so long. Kathy said she'd tell him to stop by and look at the document. If anyone could identify the languages, it was Chris.

"I have no idea," Christ said when he finally appeared at the end of the day. He had his bag slung over one shoulder, his phone vibrating in his hand.

Mara frowned. "But isn't that your job?"

Chris shrugged, looking closer at the text. "Are you sure those are even words? They look more like scratch marks to me."

"What are you talking about? Of course they're words." Mara looked down at the nearest page. It was clearly a written language. She couldn't decide if Chris seriously didn't see the words, or if he was lying so he could leave for the day.

"I don't know, Mara. Maybe some here, might be something... but all this, nah. I

mean, it might be some sort of early cuneiform, but I doubt it." He chewed his lip.

Mara knew what cuneiform looked like.
These were obvious letters. She glanced at
Chris. He looked truly perplexed, as if they
weren't even seeing the same thing. He
clearly wasn't going to be able to help her.

"Sure, okay. Thanks Chris."

He was out the door before Mara could
turn around. At the same time she heard
Kathy coming down the hall, yelling goodnight to someone.

"Damn it." Mara grumbled through her
teeth, grabbing her bag and leftover coffee. She rushed out, pulling the door closed
behind her. If she didn't leave now, Kathy
would want to have drinks, and Mara wasn't
in the mood. The day had been strange.
Kathy wouldn't get it; no one would.

Maybe I'm going crazy?

The thought had passed through her
mind on more than one occasion. She'd
tried talking to Kathy about it last week
when they'd gone out. Kathy had offered
to buy her another drink, and told her she
needed a boyfriend.

"That's the last fucking thing I need,"

Mara said, looking across the bar. Each male was more boring than the next. Whatever she needed, she knew she would not find it there, sitting across the table from Kathy, surrounded by morons in khaki pants and neatly combed hair.

Mara took the long way home through the park. She needed to breathe. The sun was sunken behind a building, and the shade from the overhanging trees made the heat almost bearable. She thought about the letters. Turning, changing, teasing her. They had something to tell her, but that was impossible. They were nothing more than words on a page. Flat, nonliving lines. Nothing else. But why had she been able to recognize them as a language when Chris had only seen scribbles? It hurt her brain to wonder.

She tried to turn her mind from the strange document to the green of the park. For a moment it worked. She sipped her coffee, listening to the birds' hushed melodies in the trees. The noise of the city grew softer with the evening. Mara inhaled deeply, taking in the cooling air. Then she saw a man spraying chemicals on the grass beside a couple having a picnic. She stopped, watching him work. The couple didn't seem to mind.

Then Mara realized why, despite the birds, the traffic, the chatter of the people, she hadn't heard the hum of a single insect – they were all dead. Gassed to death. Another example of nature destroyed by man's obsession with order and control.

"Asshole!" She screamed at the worker. She threw her paper coffee cup in his general direction. It hit the couple eating instead.

"Hey! What!?" The young man jumped up and looked at her. The woman's dress was stained. The park employee stopped spraying and yelled something. Mara didn't know what. She was already running down the path towards home. Why had she done that? Why were people such assholes? Did they have to kill everything? It was a park! It was supposed to have insects. What did they think the birds ate? She knew she should have gone straight home instead of taking the detour. People spoiled everything.

At home, Mara ripped off her clothes and sunk down deep into the rusted bathtub. Fuck, what was going on with her? Why she couldn't get it together, just ignore all the idiots and live her own life? The bubbles from the soap stung her eyes, but Mara didn't care. She immersed herself in the tub and looked up through the water.

Maybe this was it. She would die in this tub. Drown herself.

After a moment she sat back up, taking in the air. Knowing it was pointless. She'd just pass out and probably float back up to the top anyway. Even her suicide plan was stupid. But she felt out of control. She had to do something or she was going to crawl out of her skin. The stupid people, that weird book, her empty life, it was all too much. After the water went cold, she climbed out of the tub.

Mara fiddled around beneath the cabinet and pulled out a razor. She looked in the mirror, and ran a tongue over her lips, knowing this was going to feel so good. It went even faster than she'd thought it would. When she was done, her brown hair lay in a pile at her feet, soft like a nest of feathers. Mara looked straight into the mirror, examining her new self, brushing the last strands from her scalp. She felt lighter, as if she'd freed herself from the standards imposed on her, not just by society, but by her own humanity. She left her hair on the floor, snapped off the light and went to bed. She touched her cold, damp skin. For once she was glad to be alone. That night she dreamt about hellfire and wasn't afraid.

The First Temptation

I THINK I *might hate this job already*, thought Silfer as he watched the man masturbate.

The man was obese and balding. His undersized Naruto T-shirt covered his man boobs but only half his gut. The prick he jerked was exceedingly small. He sat on a couch in front of a seventy-five inch LCD screen, watching hentai. The movie must have been imported from Japan, because the tentacle monster's dicks kept pixelating whenever they slipped in or out of the badly-drawn asshole of the animated elf princess, whose constant cries of "EE-YE!" poured from the television's speakers.

Silfer looked around in disgust. The entire room was a shrine to loserdom. Massive shelves covered the walls, stocked with tens of thousands of dollars' worth of video games, anime Blu-rays, and manga. Posters of scantily-clad, suspiciously young-looking cartoon women covered the ceiling. A lit glass display case stocked with plastic figurines of girls with enormous heads, full eyes, and revealing attire sat in one corner. Even the bed was covered in anime-themed quilt covers and pillowcases featuring the heroines from Neon Genesis Evangelion, their faces stained with a crusty white substance that probably wasn't toothpaste.

Silfer shook his head. His skin would have crawled, but he wasn't in his skin; he was in spectral form, like a ghost. His physical body was down in Hell, surrounded by a magickal circle allowing his soul to wander on earth. According to the ancient Hezekiah Pact, devils weren't allowed to incarnate in the human world; they could only tempt mortal souls in the form of intangible spirits.

Currently, Silfer was invisible. He floated in front of the masturbator, glad he'd left his sense of smell back in Hell. The guy looked like he hadn't washed in a while. The odor of dick cheese was distasteful, even to a devil who'd worked in the shittiest pits of the underworld.

At least this will probably be quick, he thought.

Silfer made himself visible in a theatrical display of smoke and pyrotechnics. The masturbator let go of his dick and leapt off the couch. Frozen in fear he watched the smoke clear, until he could see just what Silfer wanted him to see – a sexy anime succubus with big eyes, a tight body, oversized tits, and a bubble butt in a pair of skimpy shorts. The man's eyes widened in amazement and lust.

"Hey sexy," said Silfer in the *kawaii* voice of a Japanese schoolgirl. "I sensed your desires all the way from Hell. How'd you like to spend ten minutes with me? All you have to do is sign your name in my book. Then, when you die, you can spend the whole of eternity with me and my sexy friends! It's a win-win. What do you say?"

With a puff of smoke the *Book of Pacts* appeared in Silfer's right hand. A quill already dripping with ink appeared in his left.

The masturbator stared at him, captivated, mouth gaping, forehead sweating, tiny prick rubbing eagerly against his fat roll. What thoughts were careening through his desperate mind? Would he reject the offer and save his immortal soul? Or would a lifetime of sexual frustration push him over the edge? Probably the latter. The guy had "thirty-eight-year-old-virgin" practically tattooed to his forehead in flashing neon letters. Silfer doubted he'd be thinking with his frontal lobe.

"I'll do it!" he said. "Where do I sign?"

Silfer flipped the book open to an empty page, where the contract mystically appeared, seared into the parchment in a flash of flame. The book became tangible, as did the quill. Silfer handed it to the man, who took it and scrawled his name on the dotted line without even reading. His eyes barely even looked at the page; they were glued to Silfer's illusory tits.

Silfer snapped the book shut. It vanished in a gray haze, along with the quill. A rusty egg timer appeared in Silfer's hand instead. He wound it up to ten minutes.

"Okay sexy man," he said. "Your time

starts now."

The guy drooled, staring like a fat kid at a buffet who couldn't decide what to scarf down first. He lunged forward, but his arms passed through Silfer's formless body.

"What?" he said, trying to grab a phantom tit. "What the fuck...?"

"Sorry," said Silfer. "But you should've paid more attention. I said you could have ten minutes with me. I didn't say you could actually touch me!"

The man's mouth fell open. He looked crushed.

"Oh, and one other thing," said Silfer as he pulled down his skimpy shorts, revealing a thick red cock. "It's a trap!"

Silfer's laugh echoed through the room. He expected the guy to start sobbing or something. Instead he stared entranced at Silfer's crotch, as though a nubile succubus with a fat package was exactly what he'd wanted all along. The man collapsed to his knees, moaning with desire, trying to slobber on Silfer's mushroom head. His lips and tongue caressed empty air. Nevertheless he kept licking, jerking his minuscule prick.

"Come on, guy," said Silfer with a sigh.

"This is degrading for both of us. But mostly for you. Why don't you give it a rest?"

But the guy wouldn't stop. He gazed at Silfer's illusory body as he pumped his meager meat. He seemed determined to get his ten minutes worth, even if touching was off the table. Steadily, something like ecstasy stole over his features.

With a sickening feeling, Silfer realized the guy was really enjoying this. He'd just been cheated out of his soul for a ten minute date with an illusory lady-boy, and somehow he was still getting off! How was that even possible? Perhaps, having spent his entire adult life spanking it to two-dimensional images of women, being able to jerk off over a three-dimensional one was a huge step up for him? Silfer didn't know whether to feel saddened or disgusted. He felt a bit of both.

"Jesus wept," he said, as an arc of semen shot through his leg and splattered against the LCD screen, where the cartoon elf princess was still being endlessly violated by fire hose cocks.

Never thought I'd be so glad to be intangible, thought Silfer.

In the wake of his orgasm the man slumped back, staring up at the devil. Would he experience a moment of regret, now he'd spilled his seed? Almost certainly.

"Is this...is this...a dream?" he asked.

"Nope."

"So I... I really just traded my soul?"

"Yep."

The man's eyes trembled. He sat back on the couch and began to weep. Silfer waited for the egg timer to go off.

"Well, this is awkward," he said, hoping for a laugh.

The man didn't laugh. Silfer glared at him. Fuck, he loathed humans. But then again, he hated most devils too. And the angels? Total douchebags. Had he ever met a single sentient being he'd genuinely liked? Probably not. His encounters with others always felt like a charade, a jerk-off, much like this one. A dull ache throbbed in his infernal heart. Then the egg timer screamed, and he vanished, off to collect another wretched soul.

4

Sworn to the Dark

THE SATANIST STOOD chanting before the altar, dressed in a black cloak and cowl. Sundry occult items were spread before him: a chalice, black candles, a goat's yellowed skull. The walls of his chapel were plastered with inverted crosses, Satanic pentagrams, and posters for bands like Watain and Dissection.

For fuck's sake, thought Silfer.

He couldn't stand Satanists. Especially that LaVey guy. Christ, what a bore! His book, naturally, was banned in Hell for being offensive to all devil-kind. But of course the worst thing about it wasn't the inaccuracy, but how dull it was. How could *The Satanic Bible* be even less exciting than the Christian one? It didn't make sense. At least the Old Testament had some fun bits, like a concubine being chopped into pieces and mailed around the middle east, or a guy with a gigantic Jew fro beating ten thousand dudes to death with the jawbone of an ass. *The Satanic Bible,* in contrast, was just blah, blah, fucking blah. Silfer had never even bothered to read the whole thing, even though it was banned, and reading illicit literature was one of his few real joys.

As annoying as he'd been on earth, old Anton had quieted down since his arrival in Hell some years back. With his tongue plucked out and his mouth sewn shut, he'd become a fairly decent fry cook at Beelzebub's burger joint, Beezleburgers. At the end of every shift he was dissected, dumped into the deep fryer, and packaged as a midnight special called Szandor Bites, sold with sweet chili sauce. *Delightful!*

Silfer appeared before the Satanist in a spooky red fog, taking the form of a goat-headed monster dressed in black. The Satanist's eyes bulged with shock. Paralyzed he stood there, then fell to his knees.

"Oh Dark Lord!" he cried. "Fiery Samael! You've come!"

"Indeed, my loyal one," said Silfer in a booming, vaguely goatish voice. He didn't see the point of explaining that he wasn't actually Satan. "I've come for your soul!"

"But my soul is already yours, master,"

said the kneeling figure. "Look!"

Keeping his head lowered, the Satanist rushed to a nearby cabinet and took out a sheaf of papers. They were homemade contracts, pledging his soul to the service of Satan eternally. Each piece of paper was signed in blood. Probably semen, too. Silfer didn't want to inspect them too closely.

"Every year on the sixth of the sixth I renew my vow," he said, holding out the pages. "My soul is yours! It says so right here!"

"I'm afraid those aren't legally binding," said Silfer. "I'm here to do the proper paperwork."

"Of course!" said the Satanist. "Just tell me where to sign!" He took a dagger off the table, ready to open one of his veins.

"That won't be necessary," said Silfer. "Ordinary ink is fine." He summoned the *Book of Pacts* and the quill. "Now, what do you want in exchange for your soul?"

"Nothing, my lord. I need no earthly things. This reality is but a lie, a flimsy veil cast across the true cosmic chaos of which *you* are the primal intelligence. I seek only to obey your will. To help tear down the walls of this reality. To erase humanity's filthy, deceiving society!"

"Right," said Silfer. "But are you sure you don't want anything? It's supposed to be a bargain. A pact. You're supposed to get something out of it, otherwise I can't technically sign you up."

"Very well, my lord," said the Satanist. "I shall accept any blessing you choose to bestow upon me."

"Okay," said Silfer with a shrug. He waved his hand, summoning a small black envelope. It appeared on the Satanist's altar in a puff of smoke.

"May I... may I gaze upon your gift, my lord?"

Silfer nodded his goatish head. The Satanist reverently picked up the envelope, sliced it open with a ritual dagger, and pulled out a $10 Amazon gift card.

"I know it's not much," said Silfer. "But you should be able to buy something with it. eBooks are cheap. Go get yourself some hucow erotica, I hear that's very popular."

"Th... thank you, Dark Lord," said the Satanist, looking somewhat perplexed.

"And now, if you can sign here..."

He offered the page on which the contract appeared in a shower of sparks. The Satanist signed it and fell to his knees, weeping with joy.

"Oh, Master, thank you! Now please, tell me your will!"

Silfer was about to tell the guy to light himself on fire or jump off a bridge, but he stopped and cocked his head, catching the murmur of words not often spoken on this plane. The harsh sound of the Devil's tongue blew through the walls apartment as if carried on a hot, dry wind.

"Master, what will you have me? What is thy will! Master...?"

"SHUT THE FUCK UP!" yelled Silfer.

The Satanist drew back, cringing like a whipped dog. Silfer listened. The voice was soft, feminine. Her words called to him. He hurried off toward the voice, vanishing from the Satanist's sight.

She heard Kathy's heels *click-click-clicking* down the hall. Gerry and Chris heard them too. Mara watched the two men get up from the small table in the corner, toss their trash, and gather their things. They waved goodbye, rushing out just as Kathy came in. Mara had no choice but to stay. She was waiting on the electric kettle to boil.

She heard Kathy sigh and pretend to rummage in the small fridge. Mara felt her silent judgement, her disapproving gaze, but attempted to ignore it.

Fucking boil already, she thought, begging the kettle to work faster so she could pour her tea and make her escape.

Kathy finally turned from the fridge empty handed. She drummed her meaty fingers on the edge of the counter.

"Mara –"

Sighing, Mara forced herself to look at her boss. "Yes, Kathy, what is it?" Her words held an annoyed edge she couldn't hide. She wasn't in the mood, but knew what was coming.

For once Kathy didn't speak right away. She opened her mouth, resembling a fish waiting for a meal to pass. Mara noticed Kathy had lipstick on her teeth. She wondered if she should say something? She decided it would depend on Kathy. If Kathy was here to lecture her about something that was none of her damn business, well then, Kathy could keep that pink smear on that yellowed tooth of hers.

Mara knew Kathy was dying to say something about her hair. It had been three days since she'd left her locks on the bathroom floor. The morning after she'd walked into the bathroom and looked down at the pile, wondering what she should do with it. She briefly pondered the idea of stuffing it in a pillow as a keepsake of sorts. Instead she swept it into a pan and deposited it in the trash bin under the sink, glad to be rid of it. One less thing weighing her down.

Kathy was shocked into silence when Mara showed up for work that day. It felt good.

"Good morning, Kathy!" Mara sang, walking past her boss.

Since then Kathy had been eyeing her, dancing around whatever it was she wanted to say. Mara was surprised she'd waited this long. But the week was almost over, and there was no way Kathy would wait until Monday.

"Mara –" Kathy began again.

The kettle boiled, filling the break room's tense silence with the metallic rattle of a loose lid. The steam escaped into the air. Mara looked at Kathy blankly, but wanted to scream at her, *Just say it! I dare you to fucking say something, you self-righteous hog!*

"Have you been feeling alright lately?" Kathy's voice dripped with phony concern, but Mara knew she was just looking for gossip, something to say to make herself seem more interesting.

"Perfect. Great, in fact. Why, Kathy? Is something the matter? That crate of books is almost finished. I've been cleaning some of those weird pages I showed you. I want to see if I can have them translated before they get filed. Right now I'm trying to track down this philologist Chris told me about. But he's out of town until next month. Something about a dead wife, I don't know."

Mara rolled her eyes, wishing people could just pull it together so she could get her work done. Her mother had died last year, and she hadn't needed to take an entire month off. Hell, Mara didn't even bother taking leave on the day of the funeral. She just came in after lunch ready to work. Before that she slipped the gravedigger a fifty to start burying the casket before the service had even concluded. She was then free to fulfill her childhood dream of dancing on her mother's grave. She followed that up by spitting on the tombstone. Now she didn't even remember where the hag was buried. Somewhere in the cemetery beside the freeway. Mara didn't really care.

Presently Mara peered coldly at Kathy. If she tried to keep it professional, maybe Kathy would take the hint and realize they weren't really friends? Mara didn't want to hear Kathy's opinion on her appearance, her boyfriends, or her life in general. She didn't want to know these things about Kathy, either. None of it concerned Kathy, but Kathy seemed to feel that all of it concerned her.

"No, no, nothing's the matter with your work. I looked over a few of the pieces last night after you left. I think we'll be able to add them to the fall exhibit in a few months."

She paused; the kettle finally beeped. *Thank Christ*! Mara poured the water into her cup, ready to leave. But Kathy wasn't finished.

"Just I'm worried about you, sweetheart. You're always alone. And when we go out, you never seem interested in anyone. Remember that nice fella, what was his name, the investment banker? He really liked you. Did you ever call him? And now your *hair*. What happened? Are you depressed, dear?"

Mara rubbed her left temple. She couldn't fucking believe this. She was a paid professional, but she was stuck here having this conversation with a woman who was supposed to be her boss.

"Kathy, what are you talking about? Who? What does my hair have to do with anything?" She didn't wait for Kathy to answer. "Look, I really need to get back. So if you just want to talk about who I'm fucking —"

Kathy's faux concern shifted to obvious annoyance. "Mara! I just... you don't have to use that tone. As a friend, I'm worried about you. There's no reason to curse."

Instead of laughing and screaming in frustration, which would lead to her possibly losing her job, Mara swallowed her irritation down. Her *tone*? *Friend*? Was Kathy kidding? Judging by the tightness around

Kathy's eyes and her tense, heavy jaw, Mara had obviously struck a nerve.

She lowered her voice and took a breath before speaking. Her words carried the pacifying smoothness one might use on an upset child.

"You're so right. I'm sorry, Kathy. Now I really must go finish up a few things before the end of the day. If you'll excuse me."

Even Mara was surprised by her amount of self-control. She must be getting old. She never would have been able to pull that off ten years ago.

In her office, she closed the door and leaned against it. Her head was throbbing. She looked down at her hands; they were shaking. Also empty. She'd forgotten her tea.

"Damn it," she said in the empty room.

Mara decided she also hated Thursdays.

She spent the next few hours propped on her stool, looking over the pages, attempting to place them in order. Two rows of five across the light table. Each carried a heavily-decorated letter of similar style. The vibrant coloring of the inks, the stark black words, stood out against the soiled edges, as if even fire and ash couldn't scar them.

She'd been working tirelessly the last few days, rubbing dark smudges from the edges of the pages. They reminded her of liver spots on aged skin. Gently she swabbed flaking scabs of mildew from each sheet with soft fingers. Bleeding stains soaked deep into the fibers couldn't be helped.

Examining the thickness of the sheets, the small frays, Mara thought they may not even be parchment but animal skin. It wouldn't surprise her; they'd used vellum all the time in antique books. Yet somehow this seemed different. She couldn't put her finger on it. It felt more... alive, almost warm when she touched it.

If she were being honest with herself, she couldn't get the pages out of her mind. They'd occupied her thoughts constantly over the last few days. Even in dreams she felt them, a strange, heavy presence so old it made her bones ache. Dreaming, she'd see a shadow from the corner of her eye, but when she turned, it was only ever those pages, burning round the edges, their curled letters looking more vibrant than ever before, as if the fire itself were drawing out some long-forgotten essence hidden in the ink.

Pulled to their dazzling display, their strange heat, Mara wanted to touch. On the third night of dreaming, she finally did. The fire engulfed her hands, but didn't pain her. It traveled up her arms, curling round her neck till she saw nothing but white heat. A dozen red tongues licked at her lips and probed into her throat. Soon they were deep in her guts, brushing her soul, telling her the words. They whispered at first, but soon grew louder. The fire inside surged back toward her tongue, eating her up from within before she could repeat what she'd heard.

And that was it. Mara's alarm pulled her from the ashes and brought her back to her room. Her skin was clammy rather than hot.

Sitting up in bed, she pulled her legs to her chest and rested her face on her knees, taking in what she'd seen. Never had Mara had such vivid dreams. Her hands throbbed. She looked down and turned them over, watching wide-eyed as the redness and blisters slowly faded away. Soon they were smooth again, as if the burns had never been.

She stared at her palms for a while, wondering what was happening to her. By the time she got to work her need to see the pages – to feel them under her fingertips – had grown even more urgent than usual. It felt almost as if the pages *missed* her somehow.

She felt a sense of dread as she stepped into her office and saw her table empty.

"What the fuck? Where are you?!"

Mara searched frantically. She shoved a priceless Gutenberg Bible onto the floor and didn't even notice.

"Everything alright, sweetie?" A custodian poked her head through the doorway.

Mara recognized Jan right away. "My pages. I left them on the desk last night. Where are they? Was anyone else in here?" She couldn't keep the panic from her voice. Jan didn't seem to be concerned.

"Oh, right over here, sweetie. I had to wipe down the tables. Don't worry, I tucked them into their folder, all safe and sound." The old woman wandered over to a set of shelves on the far side of the room. "Safe and sound," she repeated. Mara snatched the folder from the janitor's red knuckled hands. "Are you doing okay, baby?" Jan asked.

Mara ushered the woman to the door. "Fine, just fine. Just never touch my desk again. In fact, stop cleaning in here. It's fine."

Jan turned around to respond, but Mara closed the door in her face.

Mara looked at the clock; she'd stayed late. Too late. Soon Kathy would realize she was still here and want –

A gentle rapping on the door interrupted her thoughts. Kathy walked in unannounced and stood beside Mara's desk, looking over the newly-cleaned pieces.

"These are really beautiful. You've done a fabulous job."

Mara didn't bother to look up. "Can I help you with something?"

Kathy sighed, running a finger along the nearest page, taking in the heavy ink and texture. "I was talking to Dave about these. He thinks they might be a missing chapter from a larger collection. He wants you to box them up and send them over so he can compare them."

Mara dropped her brush and glared at Kathy, knowing exactly what she was doing. "This is my work, Kathy. I'm not even finished yet. I'm not sending them over half done. Dave can wait till Monday."

Kathy clicked her tongue. "I told Dave you'd send them over before the weekend. So box them up." Her last words were dry and cutting.

Mara bit her lip and looked down at the table. The pages flickered, as though they were winking at her. *You know what to do*, they said. Yeah, Mara did.

She feigned a smile. "Sure Kathy. Whatever you want. I'll get them ready to go."

Kathy looked taken aback, as though she couldn't believe it'd been that easy. She'd probably had an entire speech planned about how she was the boss, and Mara the employee. "Fine, then. Thank you, Mara. Have a good night."

For once Mara wasn't concerned about Kathy inviting her out for drinks. She felt sure that after today she wouldn't have to worry about that for a while.

After Kathy closed the door, Mara sat down to think. The thought of sending the pages to Dave made her stomach turn. He always had greasy hands and crumbs on his shirt. She didn't know how he still had a job. Mara wished she had a cigarette, but chewed her fingernail instead, looking down at the pages, remembering her dreams. How real they'd felt. How the flaming tongues had fed her the sounds that would allow her to speak these words as if they were her own.

A dry, subtle wind swept through the room. It curled around Mara, bringing an old smell of frosted earth and cinder. It disturbed the pages on the table in front of her, drawing her eye to a passage that seemed to burn brighter than the others. She leaned forward, closer, feeling the language coiled inside her mouth, pushing for release.

"Ascha i ge vaoan..." she said, her voice soft but firm. As if she knew the words, and they knew her. She repeated the phrase a second time with more authority. Then a third before stopping, feeling something pricking at her skin. Mara looked towards the door; it remained closed. No one had come in; the room was empty but for her and her pages. She could hear Kathy laughing down the hall.

Kathy. Mara needed to get the fuck out of there. If Kathy came back in and saw the pages still out, she'd take them herself just to be a bitch. Just to prove she was the boss and she could.

Silfer passed through the walls of the museum, drawing closer to the voice. Whoever it was, she'd been reciting an infernal invocation guaranteed to draw the attention of any devil nearby. Her voice was tentative, halting, as though she were speaking the words for the very first time. "Ascha i ge vaoan..." Did she even know what she was saying? She must have been reading from a book. But there were so few books on Earth written in the language of Hell. In fact, they were so rare as to be virtually nonexistent. So what would one be doing in a small museum library like this?

Silfer headed down into the library's archive, passing like a ghost through the body of a heavyset woman who laughed like a donkey being artificially inseminated. Silfer felt the cracks in her soul, but kept moving. He didn't care about her; he was only interested in the voice.

He filtered through a wall to the left, and stopped. There she was, reading from an old piece of parchment. She had a shaved head, like a concentration camp inmate or one of the Manson girls on trial. But she didn't have the glazed look of a cultist. Her wide eyes were active, intelligent. Her face was beautiful, delicate, with fine bones like a bird. A small scar sat above her left eye. Her red lips looked stark against the porcelain pallor of her skin.

The woman stopped reading and glanced around, almost as if she could sense his presence in the room. Silfer looked at the pages on the table in front of her.

"Holy fuck," he whispered. Were those what he thought they were? The lost pages of the *Codex Infernalis Futuatoris?!* If so, then this was the discovery of a lifetime. The *Codex* was the most sought-after of all artefacts, even more valuable than the Spear of Longinus and Lamashtu's butt plug. Silfer wasn't sure what information the pages contained, exactly – that was a closely-guarded secret held by the infernal council and various other upper-level demons – but he knew what the pages were worth. He could hand them over to Hell's elite for an obscene amount of money. He might not be able to buy happiness, but he could quit doing all these miserable jobs. Perhaps find a more rewarding career, one that only money and status could acquire. He might even be able to bribe his way into the ranks of the Infernal Engineers! Maybe if he had a job where he got to use his imagination he could cast off this gloom he kept feeling, maybe even keep himself sane for a couple more decades. But first, he'd need to get those pages...

Mara gathered the sheets, folded them along their creased edges, and placed them into their folder. She slid the folder down into her bag and zipped it shut.

What am I doing? she asked herself.

Logically she knew she could get fired – or worse – for stealing something of such value. But it didn't seem to matter. Whatever was happening to her felt more important. She just needed to get home. At home she could think without the threat of Kathy, Dave, or anyone else looking over her shoulder.

Silfer watched her steal the pages with a smile.

This is becoming intriguing, he thought, as an obnoxious voice echoed down the corridor. "Mara! Did you get those pages packed? I can send one of the interns to pick them up."

"Yeah, sure, they're in the room. Knock yourself out." Mara attempted to pass Kathy in the narrow hall.

"I wanted to talk to you about earlier, Mara, I just feel –"

"Kathy, I'm sorry, but I've got a ton of errands to do tonight, and I'm already late. I've had these... DVDs for ages, and if they're not back by eight, I'll get a fee. So I've really gotta go. Don't even worry about earlier. Good night!" Mara rushed away.

"But...but the Blockbuster closed down ages ago..." whispered Kathy in bewilderment.

Silfer passed through Kathy again and followed Mara. He'd learned her name from the brief exchange, as well as a few other things. She obviously hated small talk. Through the subtle tremors in her face, the flickers in her eyes, he'd seen her discomfort, her actual agony.

Mara couldn't breathe until she was outside.

"Fuck," she exhaled.

She stood there in the early evening, weighing what she'd done. People wandered past her. When it was found out the pages hadn't made their way over to Dave's, Kathy and all the rest would want to know where they'd gone.

Mara needed to think about this. She could probably blame it on an intern. The pages were packaged, left on the table. She'd kept the door open so they could be collected. Anyone could have come in there. After all, hadn't the janitor moved them just last night to clean? Whatever her excuse would be, Mara knew one thing for sure: those pages weren't going back.

She lit up a smoke to calm her nerves, took a slow hit and exhaled through her nose.

Silfer watched her smoke. He knew

he had to get her alone somewhere. He couldn't just steal the pages, just like he couldn't just materialize and stab a human being in the face. Silfer needed to make a pact for them. He needed her to give them up of her own free will. The fact she had stolen them herself meant nothing. Possession was everything according to the laws of Hell.

A wholesome-looking couple in yoga pants passed by, waving their hands at the smoke and making exaggerated coughing sounds. She blew more smoke towards them. Silfer laughed; it was exactly what he would have done.

"Jesus, cover your mouths when you cough," said Mara. "Haven't you heard of germs?"

People were disgusting. Mara wished a disaster would wipe them all out. She walked away, taking the most direct route towards her apartment. She wanted to avoid everyone and get home. She didn't like the idea of carrying these things in her bag. For a brief second she thought about getting hit by a car, her bag flying open, the documents scattering to the wind. *Everyone would know*, she thought.

As she walked and fretted, Silfer followed. Soon she drew close to a construction site, deserted at the close of the day.

Perfect, he thought. He swiped away his invisibility and wrapped himself in the phantom image of a man, hiding his horns, his tail, his forked tongue, his red flesh, but otherwise keeping his features the same. What was the point of a complex disguise?

Mara walked past the site. A two hundred-year-old church, destroyed. Stained glass windows shattered on the ground amongst the rubble. Mara hated organized religion, but even she could appreciate beautiful architecture when she saw it. *Sure, knock down a solid, beautiful old building and rebuild it with cheap ass shit,* Mara thought. She hated this city. The government. Kathy. Just authority in general. What a lousy day.

Mara wasn't looking where she was going and nearly collided with the guy in front of her. *Fucking people!* They were everywhere.

"Hey," said Silfer.

Mara glanced at him warily, but said

nothing. He leaned in close. She took a small step back.

"I know about those pages you've got," he said. "The ones from the *Codex*. How would you feel about selling them? Name your price."

Mara was not in the mood for whatever this was. This guy looked like a Satanic bible salesman. God, how did all these freaks keep finding her!? She just wanted to get home.

"Fucking, excuse me?" Mara flicked the remnant of her burning cigarette at the guy's feet. He didn't seem bothered. He didn't even seem to notice. His eyes were on the bag slung over her shoulder. Instinctively she gripped the handle tighter. Something about his eyes, the intensity. She wasn't sure if he was going to stab her or hug her. But either way, she wasn't sticking around to find out.

"I said name your price. For those pages you've got in your bag."

This gave Mara pause. *How can he possibly know?* She looked him over. No, she'd never seen the guy before. He didn't work at the museum. There's no way he could know what she had in her bag. Where had he come from? He didn't look groomed enough to live in her neighborhood, but also wasn't filthy enough to be a hobo or a junkie. Mara cursed herself for taking that pepper spray off her keychain. *Damn it!* She just wanted to go home and hide the pages somewhere safe. Why was she even talking to this guy? He didn't know shit; she was sure of it.

"I'm not in the mood, man, not today. Whatever you're selling, I'm not fucking buying."

Mara pushed past before she lost her nerve, half expecting him to grab her arm and stop her, maybe try to wrestle the bag from her death grip. She breathed a sigh of relief when he didn't do either. For once, she thanked the universe for her good luck. She wasn't dressed for a street fight.

But the guy began walking after her. His footfalls were silent, but she could hear his voice, soft and conniving. "Relax," he said. "This is just a business negotiation. You've got something I want, and I bet I've got something you want. I represent some very powerful people who wish to acquire those pages. I'm authorized to give you quite a lot of money in exchange. How does a million in cash sound?"

Silfer knew most mortals would do pretty much anything for that amount of money. Especially in a country like this, where the gap between rich and poor was as wide as the Chasms of Tartarus. This Mara woman didn't exactly look poor, but she didn't look rich either. He bet she had at least 50k in student loans weighing on her shoulders. Silfer waited for her to turn around with excitement in her eyes – but she kept walking.

"I have a job already, thanks though. Plus, you're forgetting, I don't even know what pages you're talking about. I think maybe you have me confused with someone else." Mara walked faster.

"No, I've got the right person. How about ten million?"

Surely that would be enough to buy her. It wouldn't be easy, but he could summon the cash with infernal magick, just like he could summon a $10 Amazon gift card. It was only earthly matter. Again he waited for her to turn to him, seduced by wealth – but she didn't.

"That's quite a step up from your last figure." Mara said, crossing to the other side of the street, praying a car would come out of nowhere and hit him. For once there was no traffic. *Figures*, Mara thought.

"Like I said, I represent some powerful people. You interested or not? You'd be set for life. Several lifetimes."

Mara rolled her eyes. The guy was clearly off his meds. She was beginning to regret all her inner musings on missing the stray crazy people that used to live around here. She forgot how annoying some of them could be. "Several lifetimes? I'm barely getting through this one. Please, just go away."

"Okay," he said. "So you don't want money. How about fame? My employers know some people in LA, influential people."

"Oh, like who, Harvey Weinstein? I hear he's super nice. A real lover of women."

Silfer smiled. She was sharp. "No one like that. Just people who owe my employers some favors, that's all. They could set you up. A gorgeous woman like you, with that distinctive shaved head of yours, you could be a huge star. Movies, music, you name it."

Mara couldn't help but scoff at this. "I can't sing and I can't dance. And even if I could, I wouldn't want to do it in fucking LA. Pass."

"Well, there's always New York, if you prefer. Besides, do you really think a lack of talent would stop you? Have you listened to pop music lately? Or seen that Rihanna movie?"

"Rihanna made a movie? Christ, is that the sort of shit you're into? Why am I not surprised."

Silfer smiled again. Of course, he was only familiar with pop music and Rihanna movies because such things were so often used as instruments of torture in Hell.

"Okay," he said. "So you don't want money or fame. How about longevity? My employers have access to some innovative biomedical technology. The veritable fountain of youth. I'd say I could extend your lifetime by oh, let's say, six hundred and sixty-six years?"

"*Pfff*. How about this? You leave me alone, and I won't tell the government you've removed those secret microchips from your teeth." Mara walked a little faster, but he kept pace with her.

"I'm not crazy," he said. "It's just that there are things out there beyond your awareness. But everything I'm saying is the truth. Just give me a chance and I'll prove it to you. Just tell me what you want for those pages."

Mara stopped outside her apartment building. She really didn't want this guy to know where she lived. She thought about going around the block a second time to shake him. "Look man, I've had a really long day," she said, turning to face him. "Uh, hello?" Mara stared down the empty sidewalk, but the guy had vanished. Lying on the ground where he'd been standing was a small business card that looked scorched around the edges.

Silfer Incinerator
Soul Trade LTD
Ex 666 303 003

"Fucking freak."

Mara shook her head and took one last, long look down the street before heading inside. What a weird day.

Return to Flesh

"FUCK." SILFER WAS back in Hell, inside his tiny cubicle at Soul Trade LTD. His shift had ended, and his spectral emanation had been banished from Earth. Cursing again, he counted up his souls for the day, tallied his expenses, and went to file his form with the payroll officer before heading home. He stepped out of his booth and immediately regretted it. Walking straight towards him was his manager Keith, a plump devil who just wouldn't shut up. Keith laughed like a walrus being buggered with a crowbar.

"Silfo!" He said. "The Silfster! The Silfinator! What's happening? How many souls did you net today, bro?"

"Thirty-six," said Silfer with a sigh. He

hated the fucking nicknames.

"Whoa, nice work!" said Keith, offering a high five that was not reciprocated. "You know what that means, huh? You get to ring the bell!"

Silfer groaned inwardly. In this case, "Ringing the bell" unfortunately was not a euphemism for bringing a woman to orgasm. It referred to a demented ritual carried out at the end of every shift. All the office devils would gather in a circle. Keith would give a speech and play horrible dance music. Then, one by one, the devils who'd netted thirty or more souls would get to bash a gong with a gilded femur and dance around in wild celebration. Silfer guessed it was intended to shame the employees who weren't pulling their weight. The whole thing was tedium incarnate, an abominable rite straight out of earth's corporate culture, which devils had been copying for decades, probably because it was infinitely more evil than anything they themselves could ever come up with.

"Listen Keith," said Silfer. "I'm not one of the damned, okay? I don't have to suffer in hell, I just have to live here. So why don't

you bang the gong for me? I'm going home."
He patted Keith on the shoulder and walked
past him.

"You won't get promoted with that attitude!" Keith called, but Silfer was already
gone.

Back in his apartment, Silfer lay on his
bed. His neighbors upstairs were having ri-
otous sex, slapping each other's asses so
hard their bedroom sounded like a racquet-
ball court. His other neighbors were listening to a loud game show in which the audience competed to kick John Wayne in the
nuts or burn off his pubes. It was very popular with the souls of Vietnam veterans and
Communist filmmakers.

Silfer didn't let the noise bother him. He
was too excited. The discovery he'd made
that day could change everything. Those
pages could transform his entire existence.
He had to get them!

He thought about Mara. How was he
supposed to tempt her? She wasn't like any
woman he'd ever met before, on Earth or in
Hell. She didn't seem to care about money,

fame, long life...what did she want? What had drawn her to the book? All it offered to mortals was chaos, destruction, and death.

He studied her face in his mind's eye. The delicate features, the penetrating eyes. Her words echoed in his head, so charmingly cynical and brusque. He laughed at how she'd blown smoke at those fitness freaks. How she'd escaped from her boss with such a mockingly obvious lie. He smiled in admiration at the way she'd rebuffed him again and again. It was exactly the way he would treat a salesperson.

There was definitely something different about her. No ordinary mortal would be so drawn to those pages, so utterly obstinate in the face of material temptation. He'd visit her again tomorrow and see if he could change her mind. As he thought about the morrow, his heartbeat quickened, driving his infernal blood through his fiery veins. It was a long time before he fell asleep.

Mara felt better knowing the documents were hidden safe and sound in her apartment, away from the greasy hands of Dave and the needy glare of Kathy. Still, she wasn't looking forward to work knowing what awaited her. She couldn't think how this day could get much worse.

She stepped outside, squinting into the harsh morning sun.

"Christ, you again?"

Her gaze landed on the deranged salesman from yesterday. Mara noted he was still in the same clothes, had the same smart-ass smirk on his face. "Still not interested." She didn't even give him a chance to speak before turning away. She chewed on her lip, worried about how he could know about those pages.

"Hey, wait up," he said, following her. "Don't worry, I'm not gonna bite." He fell into step beside her. "I just want to talk about those pages, that's all. Surely you don't want to keep them *that* bad. They're just some moldy old pieces of skin covered in gibberish. Why not trade them in for something useful? I mean, there's got to be something you want in life. If you had one wish, what would it be? Tell me, and maybe I can make it happen."

Mara was forced to stop at the crosswalk. She felt him standing beside her, eyeing her, waiting for her to say something. Mara couldn't resist; she turned to him. His eyes seemed to brighten as though he felt *this* was the moment; he was getting those pages. "If wishes were fishes then beggars would eat," she said flatly. The crosswalk sign changed, and she left him standing there. She smiled to herself. That had felt good.

Silfer stood for a moment on the curb, smiling and shaking his head. She was cagey. This would not be easy – but it might be fun. He hurried after her. "I didn't ask you for silly old sayings," he said. "I asked what you would wish for. What's the harm in a hypothetical? Besides, you never know, you might just end up with a fish supper."

Mara ignored him and went into the coffee shop. Surely he wouldn't follow her into a closed public space. She could easily yell *RAPE!* and it would all be over. Mara walked up to the counter. The same eighteen-year-old was working as usual.

"Just black," Mara said.

"Just black? We have a fantastic –"

"Look, I'm here almost every day.

Please, just black coffee is fine."

The cashier glared at her. Mara glared right back.

"I'll have to brew another pot. It'll be ten minutes."

"How the fuck can you be out of black coffee? It's a coffee shop!"

The girl shrugged and walked into the back. Damn it, now Mara was going to be late. She turned to the stalker next to her. "You know what I wish? I wish I had a cup of coffee. How about that, huh?"

"That's not much of a wish," he said, with a disappointed look. "But sure, why not? Here..." He reached into his overcoat and pulled out a takeaway cup of coffee. Steam poured from the drinking slit, carrying a black, bitter aroma. He held it out to her.

Out of confusion more than anything else, Mara silently reached out and took the cup. She looked up at the guy, then back down at the cup. *What the hell?* She hadn't even made it to work yet, and already the day was getting strange.

Maybe it was the potent smell, or her caffeine addiction, but she took a cautious sip. "Ouch! Dammit, that's fucking hot!" Mara burned her tongue. "Thanks a lot."

She stepped around the guy and back out into the street. Now not only did she have to go face Kathy, but her tongue was throbbing.

"Of course it's hot," he said as he followed her. "It's fresh. I think you'll like it though. The beans are very special. You can't get them around here. But anyway, now that I've given you your wish, how's about you give me those pages?"

Mara stopped in the middle of the crowded sidewalk and faced him. God, did he ever give up? It was too early for this. "Look, whatever..." she instinctively lowered her voice "...*pages* you think I've got, I don't, okay? I don't know why you think I have them, or who you think I am. I just clean books." Mara looked across the street at the museum, then back at him. "Now, I've got to go to work. Don't follow me." She turned to walk away, but stopped and glanced back. "And uh, thanks for the coffee. Yeah, it's good." She took another sip.

"No problem," he said with a smile. "And don't worry, I was only joking. I'd never expect you to hand over those pages for a lousy coffee. Maybe next time you can tell me what you really want, yeah?"

Mara shrugged. "Probably not." She turned away, feeling the slight pull of a smile at the edge of her lips, but tried to ignore it. She crossed the street and disappeared into the morning crowd.

Mara crept around corners, listening for that abrasive laugh that scrubbed against her nerves like steel wool. She thought she was home free when she finally slid into her office without an encounter.

"Mara, there you are!" Kathy was standing by the far shelves, running her fat fingers down book spines.

Mara dropped her bag, tried to smile. "Kathy, good morning. Do you need something?"

"I talked to Dave this morning," she said, looking at Mara as if trying to gauge her reaction.

Mara gave nothing away. She sat on her stool and pretended to be fascinated with her coffee cup. She picked at the edge, took a drink, looked anywhere but at Kathy.

"Mara?"

Mara knew if she took the defensive, she'd sound guilty as hell. She was expecting it. She'd spent last night talking to her reflection in the mirror, keeping her face as neutral as possible as she practiced her lies. *Missing? But Kathy, how? I left them right here...*

"Yeah, David, how is he? Does he know yet if the pages are part of that bigger volume you mentioned?" Mara forced herself to maintain eye contact. She was *not* guilty. She took a drink of coffee. It tasted a lot better now it wasn't burning the hell out of her mouth. She took a second long sip, trying to block out Kathy's glaring bitch face. But Kathy edged closer, until she stood beside the table, looking Mara up and down. Mara had a brief fantasy of throwing the coffee into Kathy's face and making a run for it.

"Dave never got the documents. Would you know anything about that? The intern said they weren't here when he came in. But I remember you saying you boxed them up." Kathy cocked her head to the side, waiting.

Mara hated lying. She prided herself on

being a truth teller. But at the moment, she had no choice but to lie her ass off or possibly face jail time. She was beginning to wish she'd stayed out on the street with the stalker. At least he didn't want to put her in prison. Even his mad rantings and mysterious coffees were more appealing than Kathy's passive-aggressive accusations.

"What are you talking about? I left them right here." Mara placed a hand on the desk, as if to prove her story. Both women glanced at the empty space. It did nothing to support Mara's claim.

Kathy shrugged. "Well, I don't know, Mara. That's just what I was told."

"Maybe the janitors came in and –"

Kathy cut Mara off mid-sentence. "Do you know what I think? I think you might have them. You were the last one with them. You know their potential value. I think –"

"Kathy! What are you saying?" Mara feigned righteous indignation and jumped off her stool. "You think I stole them? I've been here for ten years! Why would I steal those? They were just some old ripped pages, probably more folk art than religious text. They could be worth nothing. I can't fucking believe this!"

Kathy leaned back, clearly amused she'd gotten a rise out of Mara if nothing else. "I think you misunderstand, Mara. I'm not accusing you. At least not yet. I'm just saying it seems mighty funny you were the last one with the pages and now they're mysteriously gone. If they don't turn up soon, I'm afraid the police will have to get involved. And that wouldn't be good for anyone..." she trailed off, tapping an acrylic nail on the tabletop.

"Great, call the police. They can arrest me or search my apartment, or whatever. Until then, I have actual work to do, Kathy."

Mara could tell Kathy was enjoying this. If Mara wasn't going to be her friend, then Kathy was more than happy to make her an enemy. She'd witnessed Kathy turn on quite a few people over the years that had rejected her friendship. Both Jennifer and Martin had quit before the end of the year, unable to take Kathy's constant harassment day in and day out.

"Have a good day then, Mara. Finish those." She gestured to a short stack of books. "I want them for the exhibit upstairs as soon as possible. Maybe now those pages are gone, you could at least pretend to care about your job. Maybe get some actual work done, hm?" Kathy reached over and picked up Mara's coffee, daring her to say something. "Well, this smells good. I don't recognize the cup. Local?"

"No. I got it from a guy on the street."

"Ha-ha, you're such a riot, Mara." Kathy puckered her lips and brought the drink to her mouth. Mara knew Kathy's pink lipstick was going to rub off on the lid. Kathy took a long drink, only to spit it right back out.

"Oh, oh! What is that? It tastes like... I don't know. Piss. Mara, is this some sort or joke? I've never tasted anything so horrible." Kathy pulled a tissue from her pocket and tried to blot the stains from her ivory silk blouse. Mara delighted in the fact those stains were not coming out.

Serves the bitch right, Mara heard a voice in her head say. She smirked at this.

"Kathy, it's just coffee. Look." Mara took the cup back, wiped off the rim with her sleeve, and drank. Kathy watched in annoyance. "Just coffee." Mara enjoyed watching the anger roll across Kathy's forehead and cloud her eyes.

"Just finish those books," snapped Kathy. "And don't you worry, we're going to find out what happened to those pages."

With her threat delivered, Kathy stomped out.

Mara kicked the door shut and leaned against it.

"Fuck," Mara whispered. She thought about the pages back home, stored in a fire-proof lock box under her bed. During the night she'd felt them pulsating like a heart beneath the floorboards. But she was too scared to bring them out and look at them. Worried someone would see them and know what she'd done. Though rationally she didn't know how that would even be possible; she lived on the third floor. Still somehow it felt like everyone knew, from her boss to the stranger on the street.

Mara cursed herself. She should have known better. She was horrible at crime. She remembered her first and only shop-lifting experience. The extreme guilt of the act had killed her before she'd even left the store. "Fine, I took extra. Here." She'd emp-tied her pockets, setting two handfuls of extra sugar packets on the gas station counter.

"Those are free," the clerk informed her.

Or what about the time they'd arrested her for graffitiing the side of that building? "I'm correcting a spelling error!" she'd tried to explain, as the officer had shoved her into the back of the police cruiser. She'd come across the large red letters "Hail Satin" on the side of a building. She'd been turning the "i" into an "a" when a blue pig had come around the corner. Mara never paid that fine. She wondered if they'd tack that onto her sentence if they busted her for stealing the pages.

The rest of the morning Mara attempted to focus on her work. But all she could see was Kathy's accusing eyes. All she could hear was that strange guy offering her anything for the pages. She was beginning to think that might be a good idea. Just get rid of them. There was no other evidence except for the pages themselves. At home. In her room. Under her bed.

When lunch finally came, Mara dashed out, just needing to get some air. She didn't care if the day was hot. She sat down at one of the shady picnic tables scattered across the green lawn outside the museum. There were groups of people, couples, children, buzzing around her like flies on a corpse. But all that faded into the background.

Mara lit a cigarette, took a puff, and exhaled. She leaned forward and rested her head on the table. It was cool against her burning face. She didn't know if she could go back in there and listen to more of Kathy's allegations. Knowing Kathy, she'd probably already voiced her opinion on the theft to anyone who would listen. *Have you noticed her acting strangely? I mean the hair thing and now this... I don't know why, money troubles maybe? Or drugs? She has been very manic lately. I'm not saying it was her, but I am saying it seems pretty suspicious if you ask me...*

God, how Mara just wanted to get away from them all. Their stupid gossip and meaningless existences. She was so sick of them trying to pull her in, make her one of them. Fat and stupid and boring. Even in the depths of depression, that sounded worse than anything. Living in the suburbs. Driving a vehicle that sat eight people despite having only one child. Being who your spouse wanted you to be, rather than who you actually were. Mara had never understood marriage. All her friends had got married and hated it. "He's not who I thought he was," her friend Zoey had said one time.

"But you dated him for six years. You lived together for three. Who did you think he was?" Mara asked, confused.

But Zoey only shrugged. "I don't know. I just thought things would be different after we got married," she said, wistfully. Mara thought that was stupid, but said nothing, only nodded, glad it wasn't her.

Mara turned her head to the side and took another long drag from her cigarette, feeling calmer already. She closed her eyes and thought about emptying her bank account, selling her pages to that guy, and fleeing the city. It didn't matter where, just away from here. That sounded nice. *Away from here.* She was so tired of everything and everyone. Maybe if she got through this thing with Kathy, she'd do just that. Get the hell out of town and go be a waitress somewhere. Live in a shitty trailer park alongside drug dealers and hookers. Maybe she'd pick up a habit. Then just spend the rest of her days blissed out until finally one night she wouldn't wake up. Then silence.

Mara grew vaguely aware that someone was now on the bench beside her. Her body tensed. Perhaps it was a pig. Had they found some video tape she didn't know about? Perhaps someone had come forward, claiming they'd seen the whole thing. *It was Mara. Mara stole the priceless antique documents. She lied about it. It was her!* they'd cry, pointing a finger right in her face.

Please, don't let it be bitch face Kathy. Please, don't let it be the cops. Just give me a break today, universe. Even the tone in Mara's head was tired.

"Hey," came a voice that was growing more familiar by the day.

Mara opened her eyes, never more thankful to see anyone in her life. The stranger from the construction site. Not someone from the museum. Not the cops. Not Kathy.

Her words slipped out before she could stop them. "Oh, thank Christ! I thought you were Kathy." Mara sat up and took another hit from her cigarette. She could deal with crazy people; it was everyone else who disturbed her these days.

"Who's Kathy?" Silfer asked, even though he already knew.

Mara exhaled. "My boss. What a nightmare. I can't even talk about it...." Mara didn't even know where to begin.

"This trouble with your boss wouldn't have anything to do with those pages, would it?"

Mara glared down her nose at him. He never knew when to quit. "Look, you want to sit here? Then now is really not the time to start hassling me about that. Not here." Mara paused and looked around. Museum employees often ate lunch out here. If any of them heard her utter the word *pages*, they'd go straight to Kathy. Fucking Judases all of them.

"Hey, Relax," said Silfer as he lit a cigarette of his own. The paper was black, the tobacco soaked in blood that gave off a faintly red smoke as it burned. It was steeped in the tar-tarnished souls of Philip Morris executives. "We don't have to talk about anything you don't want to talk about."

"Like I said, it's Kathy. She knows those pages are gone. She's not going to get off my back until she can prove it was me." Mara looked out across the shady lawn. For a second she forgot who she was talking to. "Not that it was me. But she thinks it was. It was probably that intern, Thomas, or whatever his name is. I always see him stealing from the break room."

"Sounds like you've got a problem," said Silfer. He paused. On the one hand, this seemed like the perfect opportunity to press her into making a deal. *I can take those pages off your hands*, he could say. *I can make your enemies disappear*. All his devilish salesman instincts told him to pounce. Yet he held back. "I've got an asshole boss too," he said, not sure why he was suddenly talking about himself. "He laughs like a walrus getting a colonoscopy. He keeps trying to talk to me, as though we're friends. But just being around him makes me want to puke in his face. You ever read Sartre? 'Hell is other people.' He was definitely right about that. Metaphorically, at least."

"Kathy laughs like a donkey in heat," Mara laughed. It felt good to say it out loud.

"She likes to make me go to the bar with her, so she has an excuse to drink and gossip. Fucking people, man. I wish a plague would just kill every last one of them."

Silfer laughed and blew out smoke. "A plague, huh? Sounds good. You got any ideas? I mean, I guess the Black Death was pretty impressive, with its buboes and everything. And Ebola's pretty fun, with its liquefying organs and vomiting blood. But somehow, plagues just don't seem... emphatic enough, you know? Like, where are all the plagues that make people turn inside out, or swell till they burst?"

Mara shrugged, "Yeah, it would have to be something really quick and nasty. Just internal pus and boils. Them drowning in their own filth. Even then, I don't think that would be enough. Maybe all the children die first so the parents have to watch." Mara thought about all the overbearing mothers directing their children on the sidewalks. She reconsidered. "Hm, maybe leave the kids alone. They'd probably be better off without the parents. Just kill anyone over the age of twelve and the world would be better off. Burn the bodies and call it a day." Mara snubbed out her cigarette on the ground.

"Sounds like an elegant solution," said Silfer. "But what if it's not enough? I mean, suppose there's another world, or a series of worlds, beyond this one, where all the assholes live forever. You can hit them with a truck, set them on fire, turn their guts into linguine, but they always get up again."

Mara looked over at him. "Christ, let's hope not. Can you imagine, having to live with all those annoying dead assholes for eternity? Sounds like Hell." Mara shuddered, not even wanting to think about it.

Silfer couldn't help but laugh. *Oh, I can imagine*, he thought. "What kind of world would you make?" he asked. "If you had the power of a tyrant goddess?"

Mara didn't even have to think about it. "Flaming ruins and then sweet black oblivion," she said, standing up. "I've got to go. If I'm late Kathy is going to bitch about that too."

"I guess I'll see you later?"

"Yeah, whatever," Mara shrugged. "See you around." At least he didn't ask her about the pages this time. Maybe that was his other personality.

Silfer watched her stride off towards the library doors, wishing she was still seated beside him. He flicked his cigarette into a passing stroller, not noticing the panicked screams of the baby or the mother. What was going on with him? Was he interested in the pages... or something else?

Everybody's Looking for Something

DEEDEE ANSWERED THE door in a diaphanous dressing gown that showed off her succubus body.

"Hey, hot stuff. Cum right in." She laughed, jiggling her eyebrows and biting her lip.

Silfer stepped inside and shut the door, blocking the prying eyes of the meth heads in the hallway (Yes, Hell has meth. Also a lot of weird drugs they don't have on earth, like psychosine, street name "Billy Lee," a narcotic brewed from the souls of dead junkies; or Juggermordensetron, street name "Eddy Lee," an aphrodisiac made from incubus blood that turns its users into sexual sadists and murderers. Silfer hadn't touched any of that crap since he was a teenager).

"You're here alone?" he said, noting the absence of the other sisters.

"Yeah, they're at work," said DeeDee. "We can't live on cum alone, you know."

Coulda fooled me, thought Silfer.

She dragged him to the bed and pushed him down. A moment later she was tugging his boots off, then his trousers, kissing her way up his thighs toward his stiffening prick. It was only a few days ago that he'd been thinking about laying off seeing the succubus sisters for a while. Sex with them always felt hollow, nothing but a few moments of euphoria followed by a downpour of emptiness. But ever since discovering Mara and the pages, he'd been filled with excitement and desire, and he needed to take the edge off somehow.

Soon DeeDee was between his legs, stroking his cock, caressing his balls, licking his perineum from scrotum to ass. Her forked tongue played across the tender skin, sending shivers through his body. A physical sensation only, but a welcome one. As her tongue went to work, thoughts and images flickered through his head. The pages, the museum, Mara with her shaved head and black-coffee attitude.

DeeDee's mouth enveloped his cock, taking it deep into her throat. The sucking sensation of wetness was good as always, but there was something missing. He closed his eyes and saw Mara between his legs instead. His cock between her rose-red lips. Her alabaster cheeks slightly sunken as she sucked him. Mara's eyes looking up at him, filled with lust.

For a moment he was shocked to see the image. Shocked and yet not shocked. She was only a mortal, and yet... As he thought of her, his prick got harder. Painfully hard, as if the blood inside were trying to explode through the tissue. DeeDee murmured with delight, feeling his prick engorge even further in her mouth, thinking perhaps it was she who was driving him wild, rather than a woman from Earth.

Silfer kept thinking of Mara. Her pale skin, her delicate cheekbones, her pixie ears. He thought about running his fingers through her short hair, grasping the tender back of her neck and pushing her down on his prick until he was deep in her throat. He got harder still; pulses of pleasure radiated from his sex out to the rest his body, like headlights flashing down highways in Hell's black night.

Oh Mara, he thought.

Then a strange feeling came over him, causing him to pull away from the fantasy. Somehow it didn't feel quite right to think about Mara like this. Not because he didn't want her, but because he found he wanted her so intensely. She somehow felt too special to be just his fantasy whore.

What the fuck is wrong with me? He wondered. He struggled to focus solely on the sensation of DeeDee's fingers and mouth working his cock. But the images of Mara stole into his mind's eye, unstoppable. Glimpses of her, inchoate suggestions of her. Her psychic scent, her essence. Just the idea of her was hot. He couldn't resist. He pictured her hand on his prick, milking his seed onto her lips.

"Mara…" he whispered as he came in DeeDee's mouth, succumbing to the most powerful orgasm he'd felt in years.

"Who's Mara?" asked DeeDee, her voice

full of lusty intrigue.

"Hm? Uh, no one," he said. "Just a mortal I met at work."

"A mortal, huh? So that's your kink now? If you wanted a mortal girl you should have said something. We can go pick one up, Devil's Privilege."

She laughed, while Silfer pulled up his pants and started putting on his shoes. DeeDee looked at him in surprise and annoyance. "Where are you going? Aren't you even going to fuck me?!"

"Sorry Dee," he said, "but I just remembered, I've got to return some DVDs. I'll come back and fuck you some other time, okay?"

"You'd better," she said.

Soon he was out on the street, walking. He found himself wishing Mara was beside him, smoking a cigarette, rolling her eyes.

The fuck is going on with me? he wondered again. *I guess it's only natural I should think about her. After all, the more I know, the better chance I'll have of making a deal. And besides, she is rather fascinating for a human...*

It was true. He needed to know more

about her. Were her fantasies as black and bleak as the words that came out of her mouth? Was her soul as alone as his? Was Mara on the inside as beautiful as Mara on the out, perhaps even more so?

There was only one way to find out – it was time to take a trip into her dreams.

When Mara got home, she was tempted to search her body for scorch marks. Kathy's eyes had been burning into her all afternoon, along with everyone else's. Mara could tell Kathy had done an outstanding job of telling whoever would listen her suspicions. That pissed Mara off more than anything else. Kathy had no proof, but assumed Mara was guilty anyway. It didn't matter that Kathy was right; without proof it was just bullshit gossip. She was angry at her fellow book slaves for not seeing through it, and lapping it up like the hungry swine they were. Mara comforted herself with the knowledge she would never be a swine. If anything, *she* would be the butcher.

Mara wiped her hand across the foggy

bathroom mirror and glared at herself. She wouldn't let them bother her. Fuck them and their gossip. She looked away from her reflection and out into her room. She could see the box under her bed, a black shapeless thing in the shadows. She still hadn't opened it, worried her lie might escape and tell everyone what she'd done. That she was a thief. But that didn't mean she didn't want to see the pages, handle them. Feel their words swell inside her, ancient and warm. They'd roll off her tongue, out into the night air, sparking instantly. Their sounds would ignite a reality that people, until then, had only thought of as myth.

Mara had dreamt about the pages in one form or another every night since they'd introduced themselves to her. Each night they told her more. Sometimes in small broken whispers, other times in shards of distorted memories. She didn't know what they could want with her. She hoped when she got to the last page they would confide in her all they held within. Then she'd understand. Then she'd know that all of this wasn't for nothing.

With the lights turned down, Mara

crawled into bed, for once exhausted from her day. She was still thinking about the pages beneath her when sleep crawled over her and kissed her eyes. It told her to rest now, and for once she listened.

The apartment in her dream looked the same as her actual apartment, bathed in a late day haze. Stacks of unopened mail were piled by the door. She opened the fridge and took in the odor of long-spoiled food tarnished with ivory mold, eaten by the black rot of age. She held her hand to her face and stepped back, slamming the door. "Yuck!" she said, thankful this was a dream and not her actual fridge. She'd never get the smell out if that were the case. She'd have to buy a new one, and Mara hated spending money on appliances.

She turned, feeling the weight of a shadow hovering over her shoulder.

"Hello?"

Her voice echoed through the room, despite it being small and cluttered. No answer came. She took a step forward, then jumped back as she felt her foot land on burning embers. "Son of a bitch," she muttered, sitting down to cradle her throbbing foot. Her soles were smeared with gray ash.

Mara's eyes fell on the pile of pages in front of her. On top of the stack was the large decorated "H", washed in gold and twisted with red. Her favorite page, but the one that as yet hadn't exhaled more than a ragged breath into her ear. Now it sang to her and pulled her close. It had something to say and needed a mouthpiece. Mara felt the desire was mutual. What it seemed to want, her most primal self wanted as well.

Crawling across the floor to look down upon the forgotten languages, Mara felt waves of heat rising to meet her. Before her, she witnessed the letters distort and bleed into one another. Soon they were nothing more than a tender lullaby. Mara allowed her mouth to open and her lips to move, but heard nothing except licks of harsh blowing wind in her ears. It was only when she came to the end she heard the rising song of the surrounding city rising up above the sound of that wind. Sirens and muffled screams grew in intensity. They pulled her attention away from the page; when she looked back it had faded into the floor, nothing more than a square of black soot.

Mara sifted through the pile. She watched the phantom breeze pull the ashes from her fingers, out the window, and into the open air. She followed, wondering where it was going. Mara hadn't been able to hear what the page had said, but when she looked down from her window, she saw.

The summer sky was bruised a sickly yellow. Sharp slits of cloud wept the red ink of the dissolved page. Shimmers of fire and gold embers fell down upon her neighborhood. Mara had never seen anything like it. Pure chaos and death. Screaming diluted with weeping. Society unraveling before her very eyes. She'd never been more excited! She had to get out there and see what was going on.

Stepping out onto the sidewalk, Mara let her eyes adjust to the rapidly-fading light as the moon eclipsed the sun overhead. She sighed, looking at the ever-changing neighborhood that surrounded her humble apartment building.

The materialistic plague that had infected Mara's community in the last few years was burning away. The morning cyclists, the laughter of small children, the banging of construction had all been replaced with wails of despair and police sirens. Everything was just a little bit... different. Someone had spray painted inverted crosses and flaming pentagrams across the upbeat murals.

All the newly-remodeled houses bought by the lovely blonde couples were rapidly falling back into disrepair. Falling ash and cinder stained the new white paint jobs and burned holes through the roofs.

Walking down the sidewalk towards main street, Mara laughed, seeing someone had driven across Todd and Cara's lawn, flattening their Pear tree, and finally coming to a stop in the middle of their living room. Mara took a detour and walked up into the wreckage. "Todd? Cara?" she called through the gaping hole in their wall. "Hello?"

Mara passed the car, noticing the driver had been thrown halfway through the windshield. He'd probably died on impact. Mara never wore a seatbelt either. But seeing the shredded ribbons of flesh dotted with crystals of shattered windshield, Mara thought she might consider wearing one in the future. Not because the law told her to, but because she didn't want her face studded with glass.

"Todd? Cara? There's some guy in your living room. I think you're going to need new carpet..." She called up the stairs and received no answer. An ambulance sped past outside. Mara heard what sounded like a large gas explosion down the street. Shuffling and a muffled cry escaped from upstairs and Mara turned back, listening. "Hey guys? It's your neighbor. I —"

Mara stopped, seeing Todd appear before her at the top of the stairs.

"Todd?"

Todd looked panicked. In one hand he had a fist full of Cara's hair, in the other a revolver. Cara whimpered, her eyes silently begging for help.

"Mara! You need to leave," Todd said. His eyes darted from Cara to Mara.

"Um..." Mara couldn't believe this was happening. "What are you going to do, Todd?"

Mara just had to know, the suspense was killing her. There was no way she just walked in on a murder suicide, let alone Todd and Cara's murder suicide. She didn't think Todd had it in him. She had to be mistaken.

"Do you see it out there? I'm killing Cara, then I'm killing myself."

"No, Todd! Please... *please*..." Cara cried, her voice rising as Todd jerked on her hair, trying to reign her into submission.

"Cara, we talked about this. Do you want to get raped? Because that's what's going to happen. Those looters and criminals, whoever else, they're going to kill me and rape you. There's nothing else we can do. This is it."

"Mara, please just –"

Todd interrupted Cara by pressing the muzzle to her head and cocking the hammer.

"Mara, you need to leave," he said. "Or you can come with us. Your choice. I have an extra bullet."

Mara backed up towards the hole in the wall. "No, I'm fine. Sorry, Cara."

She shrugged and hurried out of the house. Halfway across the lawn she heard a shot, then a second one, then silence. With a murder suicide, no one would be buying that house and fixing it up again anytime soon. Mara could only hope the rest of her neighbors would follow suit. Maybe then the real estate prices would even out a little bit.

Mara turned the corner onto Main Street. The sidewalks were already crowded with looters taking advantage of the apocalyptic mayhem. All the new hip stores selling overpriced healing crystals and artisan goat cheese had been raided hours ago. Small fires burned in the street. A man dashed out of an alley, pushing a shopping cart loaded with stolen TVs. What the hell was he going to do with those? The power lines were down.

Mara shook her head. Even in dreams, people were stupid.

He nearly collided with her. "Watch it, lady! Wadda ya doin'?" he yelled.

Mara opened her mouth to scream back, but was interrupted by the shattering sound of vandalism over at the yoga studio. She looked across the street and saw a group of overweight women throwing cinder blocks through the large front window. One of them climbed through the wreckage and hauled out a screaming, crying stick insect in yoga pants. The group of obese females circled her, shoving her back and forth between them before finally tackling her to the ground.

"No, someone, please help!"

The narrow woman's cries went unheard amidst the chaos of the street.

Mara watched the scene with mild curiosity. The plus-size group descended on the woman. Rolls and folds, teeth and fists. Mara heard clothing rip. Soon the struggling yogi was silent. When the blood ran down the sidewalk and dripped into the sewer drain, Mara figured it was time to move on.

Pushing into the tiny coffee shop, she nearly collided with the hoard of laughing children parading their parents' heads on sticks. Inside, Mara stood before the eighteen-year-old barista who seemed unphased by the chaos outside.

"Here. One black coffee. No charge," she said, handing Mara the cup before she could even order.

Suspicious, Mara took a drink. It tasted oddly familiar.

"Cool, thanks," she said, backing out the

door. The girl just stared blankly, her eyes that of a subdued coffee zombie.

Frolicking down the sidewalk amongst flaming trash cans and burnt-out cars, Mara had to smile. She couldn't recall the last time luck had been on her side like this. Her neighborhood was returning to normal. Todd and Cara were gone. She had a free cup coffee.

Up ahead, she saw a roving band of escapees from the state mental hospital assaulting a group of praying atheists.

"I'm not saying there is a god, *but* if there is, please...!" one begged.

As Mara passed by, a man in a soiled hospital gown grabbed her arm.

"Here, hold this."

She handed the deranged man her coffee cup while she riffled through her pockets. She passed out a handful of cigarettes to the patients and told them where they could get free coffee.

Mara turned right, crossed the wide grass courtyard, then stopped. The museum had burned to the ground, probably with everyone inside. *The gas leak.* A sense of relief washed over her. No one could prove she stole those pages now. It was all just dust and dying embers. And Kathy was always there early. She'd probably been inside when the building had exploded.

Mara sat on a bench, smoking her last cigarette and finishing her coffee. She surveyed the fall of the city, the destruction of man. Behind her, the polluted river ran red with blood.

"Oh, cute horses!"

Mara admired the group of horsemen wandering down the center of the street observing the wreckage. She tossed her cigarette aside, not even having to worry about starting a fire or getting lectured about littering.

"Can I pet?" she asked.

The black steed nuzzled her face. This was the best day ever! The mounted police had never let Mara pet their horses.

"Looks like blood rain," said the rider on the red one.

Mara looked up at the thickening clouds, fat and crimson, like heavenly hematomas. The white horseman offered his hand and pulled Mara up behind him. As the sky wept blood for humanity, the pale horsemen dropped Mara off outside her apartment building, which was miraculously untouched and just as shabby as ever.

"Thanks! Bye!" She waved before hurrying inside. Mara opened her apartment door and stepped into hushed black eternity. "Finally." She sighed, and fell into nothing.

Mara awoke before her alarm went off, but lay in bed feeling light as a feather. The constant pressure on her chest had finally lifted. The alarm repeated for a third time.

"God, shut up."

She rolled over, dismissing it, then sat on the edge of the bed. She heard rain on the window and knew it was going to be a good day.

Silfer stood above her bed, almost in a daze. He'd seen her beautiful dream. She really *was* as bleak as the words that came out of her mouth. Her soul really was as utterly alone as his. Mara on the inside was as beautiful as Mara on the outside. No, she was even more beautiful, more beautiful by far. Not sweet, but deliciously bitter, like the coffee she loved.

He looked down at her, taking a trembling breath. Suddenly he no longer cared about the pages at all. The pages could hang. But Mara, was she... the one? The one he'd been dreaming of all these years in his most secret fantasies? Was she the exception that would prove the rule?

Silver knew he had to show himself to her somehow. Reveal himself, the way her dreams had revealed her to him. At the very least, he had to confess his true nature. There could be no lying to her, no devilish deceits. Like a brave soul in Hell, he had to plunge in without any reservations, fall into a lake of furious flames. It was the only way to know if the fire was real.

He took a deep breath, psyching himself up while Mara pulled on a t-shirt and went to the kitchen. She brewed herself coffee, even though she was bound to get another on the way to work. He watched her gaze linger on the raindrops on the window, caught the faintest of lingering smiles on her lips. She was happy today from dreams of destruction and desolate skies. Silfer summoned a coffee for himself and sat at her kitchen table, waiting for her to turn.

Mara clicked on the radio and got a cup down. She couldn't remember the last time she'd felt so good. She was actually looking forward to going into work. And if Kathy gave her any shit...

Mara got a sudden creeping feeling as if she weren't alone. A shadow out of the corner of her eye. She turned with a start and dropped her favorite cup. It splintered into pieces all around her feet.

"What the hell?! What are you...? How did you get in here?" Her voice trailed off in surprise and confusion. She looked away from her kitchen table to her door; it was bolted. Her windows looked intact. Then a thought crept over her – *the pages*. Just how badly did he want them? Perhaps she'd underestimated him.

She swallowed, hardly noticing the cut on her foot from a shard of broken cup. She thought about reaching for a knife, anything, but he still hadn't moved. He just sat there, peering at her intently. Mara narrowed her eyes, regaining some control over her fear.

"What are you doing at my kitchen table?"

"Relax," said Silfer. "I'm not here to hurt you. I couldn't, even if I wanted. And believe me, I don't want that. It's just, I've got something to tell you... maybe it's best if I show you instead."

He stood up and stepped back from the table. He took a long drag of his black cigarette and flicked it on the floor. The embers exploded like a miniature firework. Specks of flame landed on his feet, and seemed to set fire to his shoes, though there wasn't any smoke. Instead, just as fire caresses an old sheaf of paper, traveling along its surface in a rising line, dyeing it black but leaving it intact, so too the flame slowly rose from his toes, transforming his appearance as it went.

Mara stepped back against her counter. It was too early in the morning for this. She watched as white hot flames from his cigarette grew in intensity, crawling from his ankles to his face. She expected to hear a scream, smell burning skin. She waited to gag and find her lungs filled with smoke, but she saw and felt none of those things.

The fires ate away his pale flesh; the heat reddened him. Mara shook her head, frightened, but unable to look away. Like the undulating, twisting letters from her pages, he changed into something unholy and strange. Something she'd only seen in paintings and old books. She opened her mouth to speak, but her throat was dry. Questions began to consume her.

"But how?" she finally gasped. "What? You can't be...no..." She didn't want to say the word *devil*, but she knew there was no other word for what stood in her kitchen.

"Yeah," said Silfer. "This is the real me. I wanted you to know."

Mara pressed her lips together, trying to take him in. "There's no way. Just no way." She wanted to deny the whole thing and write it off as a trick, but she couldn't. It was too real. "But that would mean..." *God is real?* Mara had never even considered that as a possibility. But if there were demons, surely there were angels. God and Satan. Heaven and Hell. In her mind's eye she saw the pages, remembered her dreams.

"You want the pages? That's it, huh? This has something to do with a God versus

Satan thing, doesn't it? I should have figured. Fucking politics, even in Hell." Mara
should have guessed as much. And he was
what? Trying to scare her into giving him
the pages? No, Mara decided, that wasn't
happening. "You can go tell whoever sent
you they're my fucking pages. You can have
them when you pry them from my cold,
dead hands, devil boy or whatever you are."
Mara turned away to pour coffee. The way
this morning was going, she was going to
need a lot of it.

"I don't care about the pages," said Silfer. "I mean, I did, at first. That's why I
started talking to you. You're right, there's
politics, even in Hell. In fact, there's even
more politics there. They do that deliber-
ately to make it as horrible as possible. And
those pages, they're extremely valuable.
They've been missing for centuries. But like
I said, I don't really care about them anymore. I'm more interested...in you."

He stood there, watching her as she
filled a cup, waiting for her to turn. His
whole being hot with anticipation as to how
she would reply. Even among the hellfire,
he'd never felt such burning.

Mara's spine went ridged with fear. *Her*? She knew she'd done some bad things in her life, but did that really justify having her soul ripped apart in a burning Hellmouth for all eternity? Was she dying? Was she dead? Mara wondered if she was still in her dream. She pinched her arm. No, she was awake.

Swallowing her dread, Mara turned to face the beast.

"Wh-why?"

She hated the tremble in her voice. She'd always thought she'd be more excited about something like this. She'd read *The Lesser Key of Solomon* in high school, then spent countless nights trying to summon demons to do her bidding. Now that one was in her kitchen, she was having second thoughts.

Silfer noted her apprehension and knew he'd been misunderstood. "Don't worry," he said. "I'm not here to hurt you. I'm just... interested in you. Your dreams, Mara... I saw you walking through the burning city, laughing. I saw you riding the pale horse with a smile on your face. You and me, we're... I know you don't know me, but I want you to. I want you to see, really see me. Like I said, I'm not interested in the pages. And I don't want to steal your soul or send you to endless torments or anything. I just... want to know you. Ever since I first saw you, I've been drawn to you in a way I can't explain."

He paused, looking away, feeling strangely shy. His red cheeks burned even redder. Inwardly he kicked himself. What was he doing? This honesty thing was a terrible idea. He sounded like a virgin trying to get a date. What was wrong with him? All his devilish prudence had gone out the window. His infernal heart was out on his sleeve like a cheap cuff link. Surely this would all go horribly wrong.

In her head, Mara wanted to scream at him for breaking into her apartment. Watching her in her dreams like some pervy hellish voyeur. Who the hell did he think he was? Then Mara forced her cynical mind into silence. Examining him, she wondered – could he read her thoughts? Was he reading them right now? *What am I thinking?* She thought, glaring at him. He shifted his weight from one foot to the other, clearly uncomfortable with her harsh stare. Mara stood, waiting to see what would happen.

Silfer felt her angry eyes on him. He was definitely fucking up. What could he do but dig himself deeper? Plunge even further into the fire?

"I'm sorry, Mara," he said, meeting her gaze. "For lying. For spying. For showing up like this in your kitchen. I know this must be weird and creepy. But, I am a demon. Lying to humans, spying on them, tricking them, it's what we do. And at the beginning, like I said, I approached you like any other mark. But then I saw who you really were, and I didn't want to lie. That's why I came here, to show you. You can ask me anything. I'll tell you the answer. Or if there's something you want me to do, I'll do it, if I can. I don't want anything in return. All I want is to show you I'm genuine, that's all. I just want you to see me, to know me, the way I know you."

Mara poured a third cup of coffee, still looking at him. *He should be fucking sorry*, she thought. Even so, she felt kinda bad for the guy. She was honestly starting to believe what he was saying. That he didn't want her soul, or to steal the pages. *Damn it*. She had such a soft spot for weirdos. Mara walked around the broken cup on the floor and sat at her table. She lit a cigarette, offering one to the demon.

"So, Hell, what's that like?" She exhaled, genuinely curious.

Silfer almost sighed with relief as he sat across from her.

"Sorry, I can't smoke those," he said, waving away the offered cigarette and lighting up one of his own. "As for Hell… well, it's sort of like Earth. It'd be nice if it wasn't for all the fucking people, you know? Mostly it's just really boring. Souls have to be tortured for eternity. I'd sure you can imagine the monotony. Devils like me, we're just part of the machinery. At the moment, I've got this awful job tempting mortal souls. That's why I'm up here on earth. That's how I noticed you…" he glanced at her, unable to stop himself from smiling as he looked at her face. He cleared his throat. "But yeah, it's mostly awful."

Mara thought about this. "Huh, that's too bad. I always thought it would be kinda cool. You know, if it existed and everything."

Silfer shrugged. "Well, I guess there are some things I like. We have these beautiful storms. Blood red lighting shoots down, filled with the energies of Chaos. Sometimes it makes people explode or turn into serpents. Sometimes it makes statues come alive, turns windows into mouths, doorways into cunts."

Mara couldn't help but laugh at this. "Cunts, really?"

It relieved Silfer to hear her laugh. He felt the anxiety from earlier fading. "Yeah. People get so annoyed! But that doesn't happen often. The brimstone rains are more common. I don't mind them. You get to sit inside, see the fire raining down, fluttering on the windowpane..." He paused and looked at her; she seemed to actually be enjoying herself.

"Well? What else?" she finally asked. "None of that sounds too bad."

Silfer thought about it. "Hm, what else... Oh! and the music is fantastic." He smiled. "Actually, the music is my favorite thing about Hell. We've got all the best musicians down there. I like this band called Excruciate Rex. It's a supergroup with Keith Moon,

Nero, Bianca Butthole, and Dead from Mayhem, they're awesome."

"Keith Moon, really? Huh. I guess you
never can tell about some people." Mara
took another drink of her coffee, her mind
still reeling from the idea that Heaven and
Hell were real. That maybe religion wasn't
all fairy tales and bullshit. "So then, Heav-
en, what's that all about? Probably a complete nightmare, right? I always thought
angels seemed like they would be uppity
bastards."

"Ugh, don't even get me started on the
angels! What a pack of sanctimonious asses. And God? Guy's more up his own ass
that Kanye West. Heaven is designed purely
to gratify his ego. It's filled with souls singing his praises all day long. Thousands of
choirs of angels, going on and on about how
great he is, blah, blah, fucking blah. You like
Christmas music?"

Mara couldn't hide her look of disgust.
"Oh, fuck, no! It's the worst! I just want to
jam pens in my ears whenever I hear it. I
won't even go out during the holidays. What
a bunch of bullshit. Fuck Christmas music!
It's like the modern-day version of a chain

gang song. Just keep singing the catchy tune while you mindlessly pull out your credit card and spend money you don't have on trash you don't need! Ugh!"

Silfer loved her rant. Now *he* couldn't help but laugh, feeling more comfortable still. "Yeah, I didn't think so. It's like Christmas carols all day long. When I went there, I had to take a vomit bag." He paused, seeing the confused look on her face.

"You went there?" she said. "Why would you do that to yourself?"

"Oh, it was part of this exchange program they used to have when I was a junior devil. See how the other half lives, yeah? But it got canceled after something... unfortunate happened to one of the angels visiting Hell. They never did find the rest of his colon. But anyway, God... yeah, what a dick. Guy's a total fraud, by the way. He's not all powerful, that's just propaganda. The devils at the top could probably take him down if they really wanted to. But they don't. A war like that would crash the economy. The people in charge want things to stay just the way they are. They want the whole cosmic machine to keep on running. Just like on

Earth. Even in the highest celestial spheres, there's no escape from banality, mediocrity, greed..." He looked at her. *There's no escape from any of those things*, he thought, *except maybe with you.*

Mara was not surprised by any of this in the least. "Figures, right? Always comes back to money, capitalist pigs." They sat a moment in easy silence. "So, what did you want those pages for then? If neither Heaven nor Hell want to rock the boat, I mean, what were you going to do with them? I assume they have something to do with the end of days. Isn't it better they're under my bed than in the hands of some occultist? Or I don't know.... a demon?" Before he could answer, she glanced at the clock on the wall. "Shit, I'm going to be late."

She shoved up from the table, stumbling to her room for clothes.

"It's a shame you have to go," he said. "Can I see you again soon?" His heart beat fast. Faster than it had when he'd stood in the gaze of Azrael, or the boat of grim Charon. *Say yes*, he thought. *Please say yes...*

Mara came out of her room, pulling a clean shirt down over her head. At least he was asking permission this time; that was something. It could be worse. She thought about Todd from her dream, dressed in beige and white, skin leathery from hours in the tanning bed. She shuddered as she grabbed her bag and shoved some shoes on her feet. "Uh, yeah, sure, that's fine, we can see each other again. But right now, I'm gonna be late. I don't need to give Kathy another reason to nag me. But no more breaking into my apartment or wandering around in my dreams or whatever. Some things are personal." She shook her head, the strangeness of the situation slowly sinking in.

"Okay," he said. "No more breaking in. Though, technically, I didn't break in. I just stepped through the walls. But don't worry, I won't do that anymore. I'll meet you outside, after you get off work." Unwilling to give her a chance to decline the date, he vanished in a cloud of sweet-smelling smoke.

Mara knew without even looking at the clock that she was late. She hurried into the museum without even bothering to flash her

ID to the security guard in front. He yelled something after her, but Mara ignored him. She was more concerned about giving Kathy a reason, any reason, to harass her and accuse her of something else.

When she wasn't worrying about Kath, Mara thought about the man – or rather, the *devil* – who'd appeared in her apartment that morning. The things he'd confessed to her, how sincere his words had seemed. And yet, he was a demon. Isn't that what religion tells us they do – lie, cheat, and steal to get what they want? He'd even admitted as much. Nevertheless, Mara found herself believing him. He'd appeared and disappeared with ease. Surely he could've taken the pages whenever he'd liked, but he hadn't. And the things he'd told her about – the fire, the torture, the music scene – it all just blew her mind. She wondered if he'd take her there. Could a mortal simply walk into Hell and walk back out again? She made a mental note to ask next time she saw him.

"Mara?... Mara!"

Mara heard her name over the low hum of the morning crowd. She looked over her shoulder to see Kathy coming towards her accompanied by two men in blue. She froze, trying to decide if she should run, cry, or scream. Instead she stood silently. *Play it cool,* she told herself. *There is no proof.* She was sure this was a bluff. Nevertheless she was scared. She swallowed the fear and walked toward the trio, trying to look as casual as possible.

"Kathy?" she asked, using a veil of confusion to mask her worry.

"Mara, I didn't think you'd be coming in today." Kathy tapped her heel on the marble floor.

Mara couldn't believe Kathy was doing this here, in the middle of the museum. Kathy had an office. Mara had an office. The security had an office. And yet, Kathy had chosen to conduct this confrontation here, amidst a whole swirl of lemmings. Mara felt their gawking eyes on her, these idiot onlookers with their caftans and chunky silver jewelry, their wavy bohemian hair and big shoulder bags, all of them looking at her, wondering why the cops had cornered her. *What's trash like that doing here, anyway?* they were probably thinking.

Mara's cheeks burned. She focused her rage on Kathy; a paradoxical smile cracked her face.

"Why wouldn't I be coming in, Kathy? Did you really have to call the cops because I was five minutes late?"

The joke fell flat. An officer cleared his throat and introduced himself. Mara wasn't listening; she stayed focused on Kathy. She couldn't believe her boss was actually trying to get her arrested.

"Could you come with us, miss? We just want to ask a few things about the book. Do you understand?" the short officer asked.

Mara thought she'd do anything right now if it would get her away from Kathy.

"Is that alright, Kathy?" Mara asked. "Can I leave work to help the police in their investigation?"

By the tight look on Kathy's face, she'd picked up on Mara's mocking tone. "You know all I care about is finding the museum's stolen property. If you can help, the museum of course will be forever grateful. Take your time, Mara. In fact, take the rest of the week off. Just until we get this all sorted out." Her tone was thick with false sincerity.

"You're firing me?!" Mara couldn't believe Kathy was trying to fire her, on top of everything else! Wasn't trashing her reputation and getting her hauled away by the cops enough to satisfy her malice?

"I just think you've been under a lot of pressure this last week or two. Maybe you need a few days to rethink some of your choices. Decide if this is really the right place for you."

"Sure Kathy, thanks." Mara's words were controlled and clipped. She pictured herself wrestling Kathy to the ground and biting her nose off.

Mara felt a hand on her upper arm. As the pigs began escorting her away, Mara was sure she saw a crooked smile splinter off across Kathy's face like crazing over antique china. She knew this wasn't over.

"Come on now," the pig said, pulling her along, as if she were already guilty.

She wondered what Kathy had told them. Probably everything and more. Whatever was in that ugly, jealous head of hers.

The police gave Mara a paper cup of lukewarm coffee. Mara tasted it, then pushed it aside. A detective in a stained shirt read through his notes and began the questioning. She was the last known person in possession of the supposedly stolen text, he told her. Had she noticed anyone else around when she'd left? What had she packed the item in? A box or a bag? Had it been left laying out? Did she know anyone who'd have reason to take the pages? Did she know their worth? The questions went on and on.

"The janitor came in the night before and moved some of my things," said Mara, trying to divert suspicion. "But they always do that. I didn't lock my door that night either. Kathy was sending someone to pick up the pages and take them to another department."

"Why didn't you stay and wait?" the detective asked.

"It was already late. I had things to do."

"Where did you go?"

Mara bit her lip. She hadn't gone anywhere. She'd just walked home, alone – until she'd encountered her devilish companion.

"I was going to return some movies, but

then I ran into a friend," she stuttered, wondering if Silfer would give her an alibi. *Of course he would, he's a fucking demon.* What good was it being friends with an ancient evil if he won't lie to the cops for you? "We talked for a while," she added. "By the time we parted, the video store was closed, so I went home. That's it."

The detective jotted down some more notes. He didn't look convinced. "Does your friend have a name? An address? We'd like to talk to her."

"Um... he doesn't believe in names. And no, he's homeless. I could probably find him if you want. But... it might take a day or two. He's usually hanging around somewhere."

"Uh-huh. No name?"

"Religious reasons," Mara lied, feeling the more vague she was, the better.

The detective nodded. For a second she thought he looked bored, but it was probably just his poker face, designed to keep her off guard. She struggled to maintain her own facade of calm as the questions went on and on.

Mara exhaled when the detective finally announced they were done. They gave her a card and told her to call if her friend showed up. Clearly they had no solid evidence...yet. She was free to leave.

"Thanks... thank you." Mara was disgusted by her level of gratitude as the pigs released her. Outside the station, she spat on the sidewalk. "Fucking fascists," she said under her breath. Mara took a cigarette out of her jacket pocket and lit it.

"What was that?" a cop asked, leaning against his car.

Mara hadn't seen him there. "Uh, nothing. Just, fucking fantastic... have a fucking fantastic day, officer!" she said, before rushing in the other direction, leaving the baffled cop peering after her. Shit, what was she going to do? Mara thought about her problem on the long walk home. Kathy was going to keep coming at her. Making problems, until those pages turned up, and Mara was fired or in jail.

At home, Mara didn't know what to do with herself. She paced the empty apartment, feeling restless and scared. She looked around for her red friend, wishing he was hanging out on her sofa, or even going through her underwear drawer. Mara didn't care, so long as he was with her. She didn't want to be alone at the moment. She was tired of being alone for a change.

Mara felt her emotions overwhelming her. She was so stupid. Why had she ever taken those pages? She laid down in the middle of the living room and stared at a crack in the ceiling. The sound of rain, heavy now, rolled down her windows. The light bleeding in from outside was cold and gray. A few tears blotted out her vision, then a few more, then a few more. She rolled on her side, curled in a ball, and cried until she finally slept.

7

When in Hell...

TO KILL SOME time before Mara got off work, Silfer figured he'd better do his job, or at least make it look like he was doing it. The last thing he wanted right now was to get fired. Then who knew how long it would be before he could get back to Earth, back to Mara.

He watched the weeping woman. He'd been spying on her long enough to figure out her story. It was a tale as old as time. She was a tarnished trophy wife, past her prime. Her hotshot lawyer husband had shacked up with a gorgeous twenty-five-year-old.

She was still attractive by most people's standards. Her body was toned, tight. Her face naturally pretty. But her skin had lost its luster, her features were going slack, and the Botox injections she thought made her look younger just made her look plastic and weirdly emotionless, even though her heart was full of sorrow. She sat in front of a vanity, sobbing to herself.

"Please, God," she said. "Please, someone, give me my nineteen-year-old body back!"

Silfer sighed as he watched invisibly from behind her shoulder. Why did she care so much about her looks? Perhaps she'd let her beauty define her, and now that it was fading, she had no identity. Perhaps she'd already made her own Faustian pact years ago, when she'd married a douchebag who'd only ever loved her pretty lips and tight tushy. Either way, she was ripe for the plucking.

This should be another easy one, thought Silfer, without even an ounce of joy in his infernal soul.

He appeared behind her in a dazzling display of light resembling the flashing of paparazzi cameras and the bubbles of expensive champagne. He made himself look

like the sort of douche who might feature
on the cover of GQ or ad for an overpriced
watch. Handsome, sophisticated, rich, oozing power and the promise of beauty eternal.

The woman jumped as he appeared.

"God didn't hear your prayer," he said.
"He never does. But I'm here, and I can
help."

"Are you... the Devil?" she asked, locking
eyes with him through the medium of the
mirror.

"I'm *a* devil," he said. "But let's not focus
on me. What matters is I can give you what
you want. All you have to do is sell your
soul."

She gulped and gazed into his eyes, fear-
ful but excited, sensing this offer was for
real. "I don't know," she said. "Wouldn't I
end up in Hell?"

"You would. But you'll probably end
up there anyway. Most people do. Heav-
en is very exclusive. Your fate isn't certain
yet, but you're well on your way to damnation." He summoned the *Book of Pacts*
and flipped it open to a random page, pretending to read it. "See, I've got your file

right here. You've got way more damnation points than salvation points. With stats like these, your chances of getting into heaven are pretty much non-existent. So why not just seal the deal now? At least this way you can get something out of it. Otherwise you risk waiting too long and getting nothing at all."

"But... but don't people get tortured in hell?"

"Please," said Silfer, scoffing. "Don't listen to all that ridiculous heavenly propaganda. Hell isn't like that. It's a fun place. All the best musicians are there. Do you like The Beatles?"

"Do I look like someone who's old enough to like the Beatles?" she said.

Silfer gave her a look that said *yes*, you do look like someone who's old enough to like the Beatles.

"Okay," she said. "Yes, I like them."

"Well, they're there. They're in Hell. You'd get to hang out with them."

"What? But they're not all dead yet!"

"Oh, right. Well, the dead ones are definitely there. The others will be there soon, trust me. And Lennon was the best one anyway. He's been there for ages. Elvis, Hendrix, Joplin, you name it. I'm sure all the infernal celebrities would love to hang out with a glamorous woman like you. After your metamorphosis, that is. Why, handsome Devils will be lining up around the block to take you out on dates! You'll be wined, dined, treated like royalty. They love beautiful women in Hell!"

"I don't know..."

"Besides, think about it," Silfer continued, "Do you really want to go to Heaven? That place is awful. I mean, it's full of Christians. Ugh. Are you a Christian?"

"Well, not really. Although technically my family is Lutheran..."

"I'm not talking about lip-service Christians. I'm talking about the happy-clappy ones. The ones who listen to Christian rock and make those fucking awful infomercials."

"Oh, God, no," said the woman with a look of disgust.

"Exactly. Heaven is full of those people. All sorts of assholes. Jim Jones, Fred Phelps –"

"*Those* guys are in heaven?"

"Of course. What sort of people did you expect would be there?"

"I don't know... good people?"

"Nah. It's mostly just people who kiss God's ass. He's a total Narcissist, he loves the suck-ups more than anything. To give you an idea... have you ever had Mormons show up on your doorstep?"

"You've got to be kidding me," she said, looking horrified. "Are you saying Mormons are in heaven? That Mormonism is the true religion?!"

"What? No, I was just using them as an example. The Mormons are in Hell. We put them in a ghetto because everyone hates them. But there are plenty of people in heaven similar to Mormons. They like to wear white and sing in choirs. Basically the whole place is one big choir. I hope you like choir singing. There's no booze there either. Heaven is a dry dominion."

The woman glanced at the glass of chardonnay in front of her, the nearly-empty bottle beside it.

"Oh my," she said. "All that sounds dreadful."

"No kidding," said Silfer. Of course, he

hadn't been completely truthful in his depiction of the afterlife. But, just like a police officer trying to make a mentally handicapped person falsely confess to a murder, he was allowed to lie in order to tempt souls to perdition. The stuff about God being a narcissist was true though. Guy was a jerk. He wasn't even all-powerful, that was just fake divine news, like that nonsense in the Bible.

Silfer cleared his throat and checked his illusory Rolex. "Okay, I've really got to get going, so you'll have to decide."

"So soon? Can't you leave me your card or something, so I can think about it?"

"Sorry, it doesn't work like that. This is your one chance. And once I walk out that door, the odds of another devil showing up are very poor indeed. You want my advice? Take advantage of this offer while you can. Of course you're welcome to decline, it's no skin off my teeth. Like I said, you'll probably just end up in Hell anyway. But I'm empowered to give you what you desire, should you choose to take my deal. I'll give you one minute to decide."

The woman nodded and looked into the

mirror, glancing miserably at her Botoxed forehead, her crow's feet, her sagging skin. Longingly, she seemed to stare at a phantom of her youthful perfection. Through the mirror she glanced back at Silfer's false face, taking in his aura of beauty and power. She picked up her glass of chardonnay and drained it.

"Fuck it," she said. "It's a deal!"

She stood up, determined, alive with the fire of longing. Silfer summoned the Book of Pacts and the quill. Her contract was seared into the paper in a flash of flame. She gazed at the ornate, spidery handwriting as he held the book out to her. She took the quill and signed. As soon as her signature was down, the book vanished, as did the quill from her hand.

Silfer turned to leave.

"Wait!" she said. "When do I get my wish?"

"Oh, right," said Silfer. "Well, I'm afraid you didn't read the fine print. You won't get your nineteen-year-old body back until you actually get to Hell. But just think about it! You'll be beautiful for all eternity. And they really do love beautiful women down there.

Handsome devils will be lining up around the block to take you out. Probably some not-so-handsome ones, too. I'm sure you'll have fun."

"You... you bastard!"

She threw the empty wineglass at his head. It passed through his spectral form and smashed against the wall. He looked at her, and sighed with contempt.

"Why didn't you read the fine print?" he asked.

"I couldn't read it," she said. "Not without my spectacles."

"Why didn't you wear your spectacles?"

"Because they make me look old!"

Silfer shook his head and checked his watch. This was getting boring. He gave the woman one last disappointed look, then vanished like a flame whipped out by the wind. If he was going to meet Mara, he wanted to be early.

Silfer hovered back and forth in front of the museum, waiting for Mara to emerge so he could walk her home. Why was she taking so long? Was she avoiding him? Perhaps she was still inside, hoping he'd give up and go away. Maybe she'd even left early to escape him. He took an extra-long drag of his cigarette, tasting the soul of the Marlboro Man, sliced into a million trillion pieces and turned into Hellish nicotine. The taste calmed his nerves and gave him hope.

There's no way. It can't end like this. Mara and me... there's something here, I can feel it! She must feel it too. So why isn't she here?

Surely something had gone wrong. Maybe something bad had happened. She could've tripped in her office and knocked her head. She could be lying there right now, concussed, bleeding. Then it occurred to him – what if she'd gotten in trouble for stealing the pages?

Nervously he paced, trying to decide what to do. He'd promised he wouldn't spy on her anymore. But maybe this was a special circumstance?

"Fuck it," he said. "She'll understand."

He hovered through the museum walls until he arrived at the archives. He checked Mara's office first. Empty. He floated past the water cooler where Kathy and two other employees stood. Soul-killing boredom oozed from their eyes as Kathy chattered on, oblivious to their suffering.

"I mean, I'm not saying she's guilty, or anything," said Kathy in a sanctimonious tone. "I felt terrible calling those detectives, really I did. But I have to do my due diligence, don't I? And to be honest, it wouldn't surprise me that much. I mean, have you seen her hair? It's just not normal. And her behavior is so strange. I tried to set her up on a date with my friend Chadwick, who's a wonderful catch, and she was very rude about it. Sometimes, I swear, it's like she doesn't like other people at all!"

Silfer pushed his cigarette into Kathy's eye, wishing the burning embers weren't intangible. His infernal heart thudded with anger. So *that* was why Mara wasn't here. Without wasting another moment on Kathy, he rushed to Mara's apartment. Once there, he felt the urge to pass straight through the front door to see if she was okay. But he stopped, remembering his promise not to enter uninvited again. So he lifted his hand and knocked. He couldn't actually touch the door, of course, but he could project the sound of knocking as a sort of auditory hallucination, a sound only Mara would hear.

"Mara!" he called. "It's Silfer. Are you in there?"

Soft footsteps, then the turning of a lock. Mara cracked open the door. Her eyes were bloodshot from an afternoon of tears, her face red from sleeping on the floor.

It took Mara a second to realize who it was. Overcome with emotion, she moved forward, wanting to wrap her arms around Silfer, never so happy to see someone. She just wanted to be held for a minute.

"God, it's been the worst day."

She moved forward for a hug – and fell forward onto the floor of the hallway. She turned her head to look up at him. Had he moved? Had he pushed her?

"What? Why would you do that?"

When he didn't move to help her, Mara got to her feet, feeling more confused than ever.

"Mara, I'm sorry," he said as she rose. "I should have told you earlier. I'm not really here. Not physically, anyway. I'm a spectral emanation. My actual body is in Hell. Otherwise I would have...I never would have let you fall."

Mara shook her head. "I don't even know how to respond to that."

She walked inside, leaving the door open. Silfer trailed in behind her. Mara turned, looking at him. She was sure they'd touched before, that he'd moved things around. "But I saw you smoke. And... the coffee, you handed me that coffee! How is any of that possible? How are you even possible?"

Mara rubbed her face, overwhelmed with everything. She was getting hassled by police, strange pages whispered in her dreams, and her new friend was an actual demon. She couldn't tell what was real and what wasn't anymore. "I'm sorry, I just really need a cigarette," she said. She fell down onto her sofa and put her feet up on the tombstone coffee table. "Can you sit? Or are you just going to lurk in the doorway?"

Silfer crossed the room and sat down beside her. There was so much he wanted to say. When she'd reached out to him just now, he'd felt his heart hammer like the gongs of Hell's own inverted cathedral. He was still reeling from the sense of excitement, the bittersweet longing.

"I wish I was physically here," he said. "But devils aren't allowed to visit earth. It's against the Hezekiah pact. Only when the end of days arrives will we be allowed to come up from Hell." He put his feet up next to hers and lit a smoke of his own. "Until then, we're like ghosts up here. Which is a shame. I wanted to hold you...you look like you could really use a hug."

"Pffft," said Mara. "I don't need your pity hugs." She took a long hit, exhaled, then looked at him. "You know what I want? I want to get the fuck out of this city. Can you help me with that?"

Silfer peered at her. He wanted to tell her it wasn't a pity hug he'd wanted to give her, but something much more. But the time wasn't right, so he focused on her question instead. She wanted to go somewhere, and she wanted him to take her. "Sure, I could help you get away. Where do you want to go? Vegas? Florida? The Pyramids at Giza?"

"Have you ever been to Vegas? Don't even joke about that." Mara sighed, thinking. Florida sounded worse than Hell.

Hell. The word resonated in her head. She stubbed out her cigarette and curled up on the sofa, turning towards Silfer, looking him in the eye. "Maybe, um... could you take me to Hell? Is that... is that even possible? Like just for a visit?"

Silfer bit his lip, thinking. "Actually, there is a way I could do that. Though I would have to call in a pretty big favor from a total douchebag."

Mara shrugged. "Cool. Can we go tonight?"

"We can go right now."

Silfer took out his mobile phone and made a call to someone he'd hoped never to speak to again. "Hey Ofaniel, it's Silfer... Silfer, from Hell... What? Don't fucking pretend you don't remember me. I sure remember you. I also remember that night I got you wasted and took you to see the succubus sisters... yeah, that's right... yeah, I *do* still have the video... no, I don't feel bad about blackmailing you... what are they gonna do, send me to Hell? Anyway, I'm calling in the favor... yeah, right now. Come to where I am. You can find me, can't you? I thought you angels had special powers?"

He sighed, covered the receiver, and asked Mara for the address. He repeated it. "Got that? Now hurry up and get your lily-white ass down here. You take longer than half an hour, I'm gonna put that video on Pornhub and send a copy to your boss." He ended the call and smiled at Mara. "Okay, looks like you're going to Hell. At least for a little while."

Mara couldn't believe it. One call from a devil phone and they were going to Hell, just like that? She had about a hundred questions about how they'd get there, but decided she didn't really care at the moment; all she wanted was to be gone.

"Is it um...hot?" she asked. "Like, am I going to burn up or something?"

She thought about all the images of the inferno she'd seen over the years. Lakes of fire and brimstone cliffs, screaming tortured souls. She was beginning to wonder if this was such a good idea. But damn it, she really wanted to see Keith Moon. *Fuck it. It'll be fine.*

"Don't worry about the weather," said

Silfer. "You'll be in spectral form, like I am now. Nothing will hurt you. It'll be like one of those virtual reality games, only meta-physical. You'll still get to experience all the sights, sounds, smells, everything. We could even –"

A flash of golden light filled the room, blinding both of them. From the cracks in reality came the sound of heavenly singing rewritten in the form of a 1980s power ballad. When the light faded, an angel stood before them – white suit, long blond hair, flawless tan skin, a cross between a Miami coke dealer and a hunk from a romance cover.

Mara had to stifle a laugh; angels were even more ridiculous than she'd imagined.

Silfer blinked his eyes and grumbled. "Do you have to make a big song and dance every time you show up? You're like one of those stupid rock bands that needs a pyro-technic display to cover up how shit they sound."

The angel glared at him. "Silfer. What a displeasure it is to see you. The other angels always told me I'd regret being friendly with a demon. How right they were. Now, what is it you want?"

"I want you to take her to Hell." Silfer pointed at Mara.

Mara waved. "Hey."

Silfer turned back to the glaring white angel. "You can do that, yeah? Pull people out of their bodies, give them a tour of the underworld? The whole scare-em-straight deal?"

"Of course," said Ofaniel, looking a little confused. "You want me to scare her? I guess I could do that."

Mara looked from angel to demon, feeling a little worried. This shit just got real. She couldn't back out now even if she wanted to. She smiled an awkward smile and chewed on her fingernail, waiting.

"No," said Silfer. "I'm taking her there on a date. I just need you to bring her. Act as a chaperone. But don't be a third wheel. Stay out of our shit. And don't go waving your angelic powers all over the fucking place. Stay low key."

Ofaniel cleared his throat. "Fine. But after this, I get those tapes back."

"Whatever. Now hurry up and get her ready."

Ofaniel nodded. He glanced at Mara, then back at the devil. "Love for a mortal, huh? Maybe you're not as evil as I thought."

"How about no more talking, or I'll show those photos to the pope."

"You know angels aren't Catholic, right?"

"Just cast the fucking spell, Tinkerbell."

Ofaniel grumbled and turned to Mara. "Lie on the couch," he said.

Lie on the couch. Famous last words, Mara thought. She swallowed, stretched out on the sofa and closed her eyes. "Is this going to hurt?" she squeaked.

"No, no, you won't feel a thing," Ofaniel assured her.

Mara took a deep breath. She felt the weight of her body sinking back into the sofa, her consciousness rising above her, a heavy, endless sleep carrying her away.

"Girl? Girl? Hey, uh, Mara, is it? You can open your eyes now."

Mara blinked, feeling as though she'd only dozed off for a moment. She saw Ofaniel and Silfer kneeling beside her, peering down.

"Did it work? Am I... are we there?"
Mara sat up. It became clear right away she wasn't in her living room anymore.

"We're here," said Silfer. "This is where I live. The third circle of Hell."

Mara stood, observing her surroundings. It looked almost like her city before the hipsters had invaded. It certainly smelled better. She wondered what the real estate prices were like? Probably ridiculously high like everywhere else.

She looked down and realized her feet weren't touching the ground. She was hovering. Not just hovering, but weightless, like a balloon. She fell as if she might take flight at any moment and rush up into the sulphureous skies.

"What the...?! What's wrong with me?"

She looked at Silfer, part confused, part frightened.

"Relax," said Silfer. "You're in spectral form, like I was on earth. If you concentrate, you can anchor yourself. You can even feel impressions of physical objects. It's not like touching things with your actual body, it's vague, shadowy, almost like touching something in a dream."

Mara concentrated, trying to visualize herself as a stone, rather than a balloon. Slowly she descended until she was touching the ground. She could feel the pavement beneath her bare feet, but it was ghostly, just as Silfer had said it would be. Mara felt as though she were walking on the moon, or tripping on mushrooms on a trampoline. She reached out for Silfer's hand, touching his red fingers. It was almost like touching little rays of sunlight. She got a vague sense of substance, a feeling of infernal warmth – but that was all.

"Are you in spectral form too?" she asked.

"No, this is my real body."

"Oh, I couldn't tell." He looked exactly the same as he'd looked up on earth.

He really did show me his true self, she thought.

Mara walked up close to a nearby building.

"What is this?"

She reached out toward a fleshy flower weeping red sap. It flinched at her approaching phantom finger.

"Oh god, is that...?" She looked at Silfer.

He shrugged. Yeah, it was exactly that – a human soul, hideously changed.

Mara turned away, wandering down the crowded street, her companions following. Instead of howling police sirens, her ears were met with the mind-piercing sound of endless cries and screams.

"Fuck, that's horrible."

She covered her ears.

"I usually have to crank up the iPod just to drown that shit out," Silfer said.

"Oh, they have those here?" Mara asked. She looked at Silfer's knowing expression.

She shrugged. "Yeah, I guess that's not much of a surprise."

At the crosswalk Mara tried to ignore the shrieks of the man suspended on the pole.

"Please don't –"

Silfer ignored his pleas and pressed on his exposed, swollen testicle. The trio waited patiently to cross. Mara watched with a mixture of horror and fascination as cars passed, trailing mangled bodies behind them. A macabre sort of scene one might see at a wedding of the damned. A thud of a corpse, instead of the joyous jingle of tin cans.

They finally crossed.

"Where are we going?" Mara asked, looking at Silfer. By then the pair had all but forgotten the grumbling angel wandering behind them, looking as out of place as a whore in church.

Silfer paused and bit his lip. Where *were* they going? He'd never taken a mortal girl on a date before. He'd never even had a proper girlfriend. He'd only had sordid, casual sex that left him feeling hollow and depressed. Where did people take dates?

"Um, the funfair?" he said.

"Sure, okay," Mara said. She hated both fun and fairs. Could a funfair in Hell be any better?

Soon the pair stood before the entrance to Infernal Park, a name Mara didn't find very creative. She was sure Silfer would agree, so she didn't bother commenting on it. Corrugated iron walls, scabby with rust, surrounded the place. Above the fence was a gigantic scaffold made of bones, supporting a roller coaster track. Cars went racing around, accompanied by screaming and laughing. The laughter was coming from the devils in the roller coaster cars, the screaming from the human souls whose sensate sinews and bones made up the track.

They waited in line behind an annoying devil family. The parents were obese. The children were obnoxious. They kept picking their noses and wiping the smoldering snot on each other, or flicking it this way and that. The girl looked at Mara and scowled.

"What's a human soul doing here?" she said.

"She's probably just being tortured, dear. Don't stare, it's rude."

The child continued to stare at her anyway, before finally losing interest. The mother gave Silfer a judgmental glance, as if to say, *are you actually taking a human soul on a date? You degenerate weirdo.*

They finally passed through the gates, stopping at the ticket booth shaped like a gaping mouth. Silfer slid a wad of cash over to the pimpled adolescent devil who manned the booth.

"Thank you, sir," said the attendant with a breaking voice. "I'll just get your tickets."

He walked over to a dreadlocked hunchback chained to a bed of nails. The hunchback's hideous hump was covered with neat square tattoos, all of which read ***Infernal Park–Admit One***. Taking a rusty pizza cutter, the attendant began, with great effort, to slice along the dotted lines until two strips of flesh – two "tickets" – were carved from the screaming man's back.

With bloody tickets in hand, Silfer guided Mara through the turnstiles and into the funfair itself. There was a booth selling fairy floss, or rather devil floss, as red as blood and filled with traces of brain. A filthy little hippie with a Swastika carved in his forehead sat above a tank of simmering acid. A giant Ferris wheel loomed over all, made from broken bones and the skulls of giant Hell beasts. There was a ghost train with actual ghosts in it, though it didn't have much of a line. Such things weren't very novel in Hell.

Mara glanced around as they walked, amazed at how similar things were to Earth. The people, just as repulsive. The rides and games, just as overpriced. This is what she'd come all the way down here for? She scowled at the dead goldfish rotting in tiny bowls as they passed. Moans and shouts assaulted them from all sides. Blood, greasy food, cigarettes, and vomit perfumed the air. The whole thing reminded Mara of New Orleans during Mardi Gras.

"So," said Silfer, rubbing the back of his neck nervously. He was starting to wonder if this was the best choice of location for their first real date. "Do you want to go on any of the rides? Play any of the games? I mean, you're intangible, of course, but I could play for you..."

"Um..." Mara didn't want to be a bitch. She'd been on plenty of bad dates, usually with people she didn't even like. At least he was trying. That was something.

"How about that one?" Mara pointed over to a dart game. "How's your aim?"

As the pair walked over, Mara saw that the targets in the dart game were actual human heads, each begging for mercy.

"Is that Stalin?" She asked, leaning forward to get a better look. "Get him."

"Sure."

Silfer picked up a handful of darts. He threw the first, nailing a head just to the right of Stalin in the eye. It cringed; Stalin laughed. Then Silfer landed a dart in his gaping mouth. The dictator's head gagged, attempting to spit it out.

Mara clapped and jumped up and down. *Awesome.*

"Winner!" The peg-legged carnie called.

Mara was expecting a teddy bear or a glass unicorn, so when the carnie ripped Stalin's head from the wall and handed it over, Mara stood there, thankful she couldn't actually hold anything.

"Better let what's-his-face carry it," she said, gesturing to the awkward angel behind them. He looked away, pretending not to hear.

Mara decided she'd had enough of darts. "So what next?"

"Oh, how about a shooting game?" said Silfer.

He led her over to a brightly colored tent. Tables sat at the front, covered with virtually every type of murderous projective weapon a person could imagine. Most of them Mara recognized from Earth, but some seemed unique to Hell. A few dozen feet away from the tables were the targets. As expected, the targets were human souls, tied up or nailed to wooden boards. Mara thought they looked vaguely familiar.

"Hey," she said. "Isn't that the guy who played Moses in that stupid bible movie?"

Silfer shrugged. He never watched biblical movies. Unless they were X-rated.

"It is him!" she said.

The guy was tied to a post with barbed wire. Someone had removed his cold dead hands, leaving only ragged stumps.

"Shoot him," Mara said.

Silfer shrugged and smiled. "Whatever you say. What weapon?"

Mara perused the murderous arsenal, settling on a spear gun with a barbed spear already loaded. "That one."

"Okay. Here, you can guide my aim…"

He slid some Hell cash to the toothless carny devil behind the table, then raised the spear gun and aimed. Mara stood close, her spectral hands on his, feeling a ghostly impression of his body against hers. She could feel, ever so dimly, the beating of his demonic heart, distant and soft, like the wings of a moth.

"Now!" she yelled.

Silfer laughed, pulled the trigger, and skewered Heston through the family jewels. He screamed and flailed against the post,

then screamed even more when the carny devil ripped out the spear, removing his
mangled genitalia with it.

Silfer grinned at Mara. "I think maybe
you should have been a devil. Have you ever
felt like you were born on the wrong plane
of existence?"

"All the time," she grinned.

"Pick a prize," said the carny. "A prize
for the lovely lady."

"What do you want this time?" said Silfer, pointing at the prize wall. "I can make it
materialize back on earth, like I did with the
coffee, so you can keep it."

Mara stared at the assorted carnival trash. There was a satanic teddy bear
stuffed with real human hair. A cat-o'-
nine-tails. A monstrous dildo that looked
like something out of H. P. Lovecraft erotic fan-fiction. Halloween masks made from
preserved human skin. One of those stupid
baseball caps with whirling propeller blades
on the top.

"I need that bear." Her eyes narrowed
in on the stuffed creature with hair pushing
out through the seams of its face. Its eyes
were crooked, one glowing a faint red. She

was almost sure its teeth were real.

"Here, carry this." Silfer tossed the bear at the angel, who was already lugging Stalin's gagging head. "So, what next?"

The pair wandered away from the games. A head and a possessed bear were enough for Mara.

"How about the Ferris wheel?" he asked.

They stopped in the shadow of the looming death wheel. Mara gulped; she hated heights. But she hated people knowing she was scared of something even more.

"Sure..."

"Cool."

Silfer paid, and the two sat in one of the passenger cars.

Mara looked around. This wasn't so bad. No, she could do this. No big deal. If she could go in an airplane, or ride in a glass elevator, she could fucking do this. After all, she was in Hell, what had she thought it was going to be like? All rainbows and ponies? Hugging and skipping through a field?

The ride jolted to life. Rusted gears and dry bones rubbed against one another. Mara jumped in her seat.

"Shit," she gasped, trying to reach out

for Silfer's hand, but once again unable to grasp him. She looked down. "Oh, sorry," she said, feeling dumb, as if her puny mortal mind just couldn't get it.

He looked at her, understanding.

"No, you're fine," he assured her, wishing he too could reach out and touch her.

Mara looked down at her feet as the ride climbed higher. Soon they were towering over the crowds. The gears creaking, the seats rocked back and forth. Mara knew this was how she was going to die, right here, in Hell, on this rusted-out fucking Ferris wheel.

"You okay?" Silfer asked, noticing Mara looked kinda sick.

"Yeah, sure. Just great," she said, her words flat and concentrated. If she wasn't careful, she might start screaming and be unable to stop.

"You're lying," he said. Clearly she was *not* having a good time.

"No, no, it's fine. We did what I wanted. So I can do this. I just, uh..." she looked at him from the corner of her eye. "I'm really fucking terrified of um... heights." She practically whispered the words, feeling more pathetic than ever.

"Oh, shit," said Silfer. "Why didn't you say anything? Well, they won't let us off now. Here, maybe you should just lean into me. I know we can't really touch, but..."

He put his arms around her spectral form, guiding her phantom body closer to his chest. He could just barely feel her, like a field of static, or a spider's web stretched across a midnight lane, brushing the skin. Except she felt infinitely better than either of those things. A tingle of excitement ran through him. Even like this, her presence felt wonderful. If only she were here in the flesh.

Mara closed her eyes and leaned into him, taking in a deep breath. Despite the absence of her physical body, she could almost feel his, just so, a soul lingering close. It was reassuring; she wasn't going to fly into a million pieces. For a moment, Mara almost forgot she was so far above the ground. How good it would have felt if she were there completely in the flesh. Solid. Whole. Feeling the weight of his arm draped across her shoulder, keeping the wolves of fear from the door of her mind.

Mara found herself shocked by some of these thoughts. She normally hated everyone. She'd loathed all the men she'd ever dated. In fact, on most of her dates she would have preferred to have been in spectral form. It would have saved her from a lot of awkward goodnight kisses and hungry hands.

The Ferris wheel ground to a dead stop, shaking the seat back and forth, but Mara hardly noticed.

"Hey!" shouted the carny operator. "Ride's over, lovebirds! Pay for another turn or get off!"

Silfer and Mara looked up, both of them awoken from a trance. They hurried off the ride. Standing in the wheel's shadow, Silfer was glad he was wearing his overcoat; holding Mara close, even spectral Mara, had gotten him excited in more ways than one.

"So," he said, rubbing the back of his neck again. "I'm kinda thinking maybe the fairground wasn't such a great idea. I'm sorry, it's just, well, I don't really go on dates. Maybe we could head somewhere else?"

"Okay," said Mara. Torturing Stalin and Heston had been fun. Even the Ferris wheel had turned out to be surprisingly good. But the annoying fairground ambiance definitely wasn't to her liking. "What did you have in mind?"

Silfer glanced away, his eyes full of excitement.

"Holy fuck," he said. "Did you hear that?"

"Hear what?" Mara hadn't heard anything other than the same ceaseless deluge of screaming.

"This way!"

He rushed off, pushing his way through the crowd, knocking a demonic teenager right on her ass.

"Watch out, shithead!" the girl cried.

Silfer ignored her and followed the voice he'd heard before.

"Excruciate Rex... Exclusive gig..."

The voice came from a devil in an overcoat and cowl. He looked like the sort of guy who spent his days masturbating on the subway and his nights sniffing glue. People avoided him as he tried to hand out poorly-photocopied flyers covered in the almost-unreadable logo of the avant-garde black metal insanity band known as Excruciate Rex.

Silfer yanked one of the flyers from his hand and held it out to Mara.

"Holy shit," he said. "I can't believe it! It's my favorite band, the one I was telling you about. I've been wanting to see them for years, but I've never had a chance. They almost never perform live. And when they do, they keep it a secret until right on the day. Then they publicize it really poorly, so almost no one knows about it! And they only play in the sleaziest, most obscure dive bars. But they're playing in half an hour!" He looked at her, eyes wild with excitement. "Isn't this the craziest coincidence? My favorite band playing, on the same day I bring you to Hell? It's like it was all meant to be!"

They came to a hole in the wall club, as filthy as anything Mara had seen. It looked like it should have been condemned, a cross between a junkie squat and a charnel house, except that those places probably smelled better.

"Well?" Silfer asked, looking over at Mara.

"I love it," she beamed, watching a beast come wandering out, a syringe jammed in his neck. He passed out inches from her boots. The pair stepped over him and into the darkness of the building. As they descended the steps into a basement the music grew louder, drowning out the horribleness of the city. By now Mara felt fully immersed in the sights and sounds of Hell, forgetting, at least for the moment, her problems on Earth.

The basement – which was technically more of an underground cavern – had stalactites on the ceiling resembling rows of murderous teeth. Oversized bats nested amongst them, looking languid despite the crashing music. Eerie red lights shone through billowing smoke, illuminating a trio of figures on the stage.

"Is that them?" yelled Mara.

"What?"

"IS THAT THEM!?"

"No! That must be the supporting act!" Silfer yelled back, inches from Mara's ear.

They headed deeper inside, passing merch tables manned by stoned roadettes smoking cigarettes and looking perennially sleep deprived. The table was a clutter of CDs, records, and T-shirts emblazoned with the band's unreadable, ridiculous logo, plus a series of jars with labels like "Nero's Blood," "Nero's Semen," and "Nero's special Bathwater." Beyond the merch table was a bar where hordes of devils lined up for drinks. There were bottles with eyeballs and serpents floating inside.

Mara scanned the crowd. They looked rough, weird. There were demonic metal-heads, bikers, druggies, all sorts of unsavory characters. Mara was impressed. She'd been worried for a second Silfer might have over-hyped the music scene in an attempt to make Hell sound cooler than it actually was. More than once she'd had been dragged to a concert under the guise of seeing a "good" band, only to end up trapped in the middle of a thousand idiots, all of them watching one pretentious idiot prancing around be-hind a shadowy curtain. No, Mara could get used to this.

The music stopped as the singer on stage was brained with a crumbling brick.

"Excruciate Rex!!" someone roared.

The crowd chanted, "Rex! Rex! Rex!"

The opening band fled as bottles, bricks, and a severed penis were hurled in their direction. The curtains dropped, and the music of lyres poured from the speakers, which looked like nothing less than severed human heads bound with sinews, their mouths perpetually open, unleashing hellish sounds.

"Oh shit, this is it!" said Silfer. "They always come on to the music of Lyres. Come on, let's get a good spot!"

He led Mara towards the mosh pit. The angel followed, lugging Stalin's head and the Satanic teddy bear, looking woefully out of place.

Silfer waited in tense anticipation. He reached out, taking Mara's spectral hand in his. He could hardly feel her, but it was better than nothing. He turned to her and smiled, so full of excitement. To think - his favorite band, and his favorite person, here in one place!

I hope she likes them as much as I do, he thought.

Mara felt the reassuring, warm presence of Silfer's hand close to hers. She wanted to close her fingers around his, but knew it was pointless to want what wasn't possible.

No, she thought. She wasn't going to let those thoughts in, those doubts. She was here to have a good time and forget about all that, at least for now. She'd have plenty of time for self-loathing and gloom back on earth.

Torturous moments dragged on. The crowd chanted. Smoke coiled and cavorted amongst the sweaty bodies. The lights changed from red to eerie green. Finally the curtains parted, drawing a roar of excitement from the devilish throng.

Dead appeared, slathered in corpse paint. Ragged brains peeked through the hole he had blown in his skull. He grinned at the audience as he strode the cramped stage. The crowd screamed when they saw him reach up and scoop out some brain. He tossed little bits to the crowd as though feeding sharks some chum. Members of the audience grabbed the pink morsels and gobbled them down, shouting for more.

Nero stepped out next, wearing his iconic chin beard. A black laurel crown sat above his fat, corpse-painted face. He wore a black toga woven from the silk of the finest Hell worms. Spectral flames danced in a nimbus around his guitar. Then came Bianca Butthole, carrying her bass, her skinny frame festooned with the finest Hell tattoos. Finally, Keith Moon appeared and staggered to the drum kit.

"I can't fucking believe it. He looks so young!" Mara said in awe.

Clearly as high as a kite, Keith tripped and fell behind his drum kit. Crawling the rest of the way, he finally climbed onto his throne and located his sticks. The crowd cheered. Keith looked confused, as if trying to figure out who he was, where he was, and what he was supposed to be doing. After a moment he began banging out the opening song with clear, unrestrained enthusiasm.

"This is going to be amazing!" Mara jumped and down, never more excited. All the bands she loved were dead, and a few of their members were right fucking here. "I'm having the best time!" She screamed in Silfer's ear. For once, she was telling the truth.

Mara's words were even more beautiful to Silfer's ears than the sound of the opening song. Reflexively he tried to squeeze her hand, but his fingers passed through hers.

He put his arm around her nevertheless, savoring her presence, however ghostly. Together they listened in rapturous joy as Excruciate Rex played their first four songs – "Pig Head Molestation," "Festering Waters of Lethe," "Implantation/Infestation," and "Crystallized Agony Condemned." Maniac drumbeats and phantasmagoric riffs washed over the crowd, while Dead, Nero and Bianca took turns singing the eerie, oft incomprehensible lyrics.

"You're right," said Mara. "This band is wicked cool!"

A shower of blood and teeth flew through her spectral face. She turned to see some demonic skinheads in acid wash jeans beating the shit out of a stoned human soul in the middle of the mosh pit. The bouncers moved in, but the bloodshed only intensified.

"Wow. So, uh, this is getting a bit intense," said Mara, noticing the smoke machines weren't machines at all, but burning Christians in tight steel cages. The crowd responded to the carnage with more enthusiasm. Demons started ripping their clothes off, slathering themselves in gore. Acts of indiscriminate coupling began. Soon devils were fucking on the floor, on the tables, up against the walls.

Mara looked to her left, observing a she-beast sucking a devil's dick. As the devil moaned with pleasure, his tail whipped out towards Mara, slithering along her thankfully intangible ass as though looking for an opening. Silfer put his cigarette out on the tip of the rude devil's tail.

"Fuck off," he said.

The tail recoiled. Mara and Silfer huddled closer.

That's when the vomiting started. Nero had been chowing down on whole buckets of Szandor bites since the set had begun, chasing them down with flagons of wine. His belly hideously distended, he stumbled to the edge of the stage and unleashed a stream of vomit across the audience in front. He held the mic to his mouth as the spew was unleashed; the sound of his retching, thunderous and wet, merged with the music.

Instead of recoiling, the devils in the front row laughed, smearing the puke with the blood, cum, and sweat that already covered their bodies. Some began to vomit in turn, until the front of the mosh was a sickening mire, in which the crowd continued to fuck indiscriminately, using fingers, tongues, tails, even discarded glassware.

"I think I've had enough music for one evening!" Mara yelled over the clamor of sex and heavy metal.

"Me too!" said Silfer as they pushed their way towards the exit. The angel followed them outside, grumbling about all the semen in his fabulous hair.

"What did I tell you about talking?" snapped Silfer. "And walk downwind, you smell fucking awful. I hope you don't let any of that shit get on the teddy bear."

The angel fell silent. Silfer turned to Mara as they stood beneath Hell's bloody moon. His ears were ringing, his heart pounding. Her face in the moonlight, luminous and red, was the greatest sight he'd ever seen.

"So," he said. "What did you think? I mean, before all the puking."

Mara couldn't believe he was even asking her that. She thought the answer was clear. "Fucking awesome! The only band

I've ever seen like that was Temperance Holocaust, but even they didn't puke on everyone, just bled. Oh, and they were all alive. But performance wise, the intensity, I guess…" Mara trailed off. She noticed she was rambling, and bit her tongue. She couldn't remember the last time she'd had so much fun, let alone with another person. Hell, she couldn't remember the last time she'd talked so much. She really didn't want to go back to Earth.

The pair continued to walk in comfortable silence. Mara sighed. "So Hell isn't as bad as I'd thought it would be. At least Kathy isn't here." Mara hated saying her name. Even in Hell she couldn't escape the lingering fear that her boss was going to fire her, or worse, get her put in jail.

Silfer laughed at her joke, but sensed the concern underneath. "Don't worry about that bitch," he said. "We can —"

"Excuse me," said the angel, drawing closer.

"What?!" snapped Silfer, turning, flashing his fangs in anger.

"I think I've had enough of being in Hell," said Ofaniel. "That debt of ours is just about repaid. It's time for me to take this mortal back."

"Not yet," said Silfer, a beat of panic in his chest. "I still..." he glanced around, catching sight of the river Styx nearby. "I still have to take her for a walk on the beach!" He turned to Mara. "Sound good?"

Mara normally hated the beach, but everything seemed better in Hell. "Yeah, sure."

The angel grumbled as Silfer held Mara's spectral hand and led her towards the river. They passed the crumbling stone wall and found themselves on a beach of ashes and bone. Bloody waves washed against a mound of human skulls, steadily beating them to powder. College-age demons drank and fornicated beside a bonfire.

Mara stepped on a dirty syringe. "Some things never change. Glad I'm intangible." She paused, catching the needful look on Silfer's face. "I mean, I'm glad I'm intangible for some reasons. Not for others..." Her smile was bittersweet. "So, if we were to... be together, how would it work? With me on Earth, you in Hell, this whole intangibility thing..."

"Well, I guess, you would have to die. Which will happen eventually, right? Then your soul could come down here. I could use my Devil's Privilege to claim you as my own. You could live with me. I'd have to pretend I was torturing you, of course, otherwise it might ruin my reputation. Devils aren't supposed to fall... aren't supposed to have feelings for mortals. So you might have to scream and moan at night, for the benefit of the neighbors."

"I think I might be able to manage that last part," said Mara. "But dying...it's a big step."

"Don't worry about that now. Let's just enjoy what we have."

They wandered along the shore in hushed serenity.

"Ah, fuck! Get off of me, you brutes!"

They turned to see the angel running from a monstrous seagull intent on eating the demonic jism from his Fabio hair.

"That's it!" said Ofaniel. "This is over! I'm getting the fuck out of here! Say goodbye to your date, Silfer. And don't ever fucking call me again!"

The couple turned to one another as the

angel began the incantation. Mara cringed at the thought of going back to Earth, her own very real Hell.

"Christ, I don't know. Maybe given the choice between dealing with Kathy or dying, dying sounds like a better alternative," Mara said, reviewing her options.

"Hey, don't worry about Kathy," said Silfer. "I've got a plan to get her out of your hair for good. Just go to work tomorrow as usual, and it'll all be taken care of."

Mara felt that sounded too good to be true. "What are you going to do?"

She never heard the answer. She opened her eyes the next morning in bed. For a moment she wondered if she'd dreamt the whole thing. Rolling over to shut off her buzzing clock, she saw the demonic teddy bear sitting on her nightstand, staring at her. She ran a finger over the bristly hair, touched the glaring red eye. She leaned back and looked at the ceiling. Of course it hadn't been a dream. Her evening in Hell had been better than anything she could have thought up.

8

She Had It Coming

"WHAT'S SHE DOING here?"

"Isn't she supposed to be on leave?"

Mara heard the whispers as she strode into work the next day. People glanced at her warily, but nodded politely, as frightened sheep tended to do. Mara met their eyes as she walked, pretending nothing had happened. She heard Kathy before she saw her, lumbering like a pantsuit behemoth from some poor employee's office. Kathy stepped out into the corridor, guffawing, then turned, saw Mara, and froze. A look of surprise, then anger, fell over her saggy face. She marched towards Mara and stopped a few feet away, whispering just loud enough that everyone could hear.

"Mara, what are you doing here?" she said. "I thought I told you to take the week off. Didn't you –" Kathy paused mid-sentence. Mara waited for her to go on, but Kathy remained still, looking confused.

"Kathy?"

Mara watched her boss's face twitch, as though she were having a seizure. Mara inhaled a scent of melting wax, burning bones, brimstone. Then Kathy's convulsions stopped and her face relaxed, going back to normal, but not quite. There was something very uncharacteristic and odd about her expression. She looked mischievous, almost devilish. She smiled at Mara softly, and winked.

"I have an announcement to make!" shouted Kathy as she stepped back from Mara. "Everyone gather round! Listen up!" She clapped her hands, put her fingers between her lips and gave a loud whistle.

Reluctantly, Mara's colleagues rose from their desks or shuffled from their offices, all looking distinctly apathetic about having to listen to what they no doubt assumed would be another of Kathy's inept motivational speeches or workplace lectures. Kathy seemed annoyed by everyone's lack of enthusiasm. She zeroed in on two men whispering off to the side. Without warning she barged towards them, landing a slap across one's face.

"I said fucking listen to me!" she yelled.

The employee, a jowly bald guy called Brian that Mara had always studiously avoided talking too, stumbled backwards, his cheek turning red, his eyes stunned by the sudden violence. People stared at Kathy with shocked faces. The room became silent, all save for Kathy.

"I said listen! Fucking LISTEN!" Kathy scrambled up onto a desk, kicking aside a monitor, sending it smashing to the ground. "Everyone!" she said. "I have an announcement to make. There's something you all need to know." She paused, scanning the room, making sure all eyes were upon her. Jaws hung open. Everyone seemed certain she was having some sort of epic meltdown. The intern, Thomas, standing at the back, took out his phone to film the proceedings, perhaps hoping to post the footage on YouTube, or, better yet, on www.madbosseslosingtheirshit.com.

"I know there have been a lot of rumors flying around lately about those missing pages," said Kathy. "A lot of you think Mara is the culprit. I know – I helped spread those rumors! I couldn't help it. Ever since Mara rejected me, I've been filled with anger towards her." She paused as if to let her words sink in. No one dared speak.

"That's right," she continued. "I'm in love with Mara! How could I not be? She's so cool, so clever, so *sexy*. I've been trying to get into her pants since the moment she started working here. She could've reported me for sexual harassment a hundred times! But she didn't. She was always too kind, too empathetic. She kept urging me to seek psychological help. But I didn't listen. I kept trying to get my hands on that sweet ass!"

Kathy closed her eyes, scrunched up her face, and flexed her fingers, as though she were imagining grabbing Mara's rump and squeezing it tightly. One of Mara's colleagues, Gerry, spat his coffee across his desk in a moment of astonishment. Everyone else stared with wide eyes. A few started giggling, smiling involuntarily, looking like they wouldn't mind a big bag of popcorn to go with this wild entertainment. Thomas kept filming, his eyes filled with joy, as though he knew this was the best video www.madbosseslosingtheirshit.com was ever going to get.

"But of course she kept rejecting me," said Kathy. "For who would ever want me?" Her eyes trembled with tears. "Can you imagine what it's like to look like a marshmallow? To laugh like a farm animal being molested by a hillbilly? To have a cunt that smells like blue vein cheese left out in the sun?! Of course she didn't want me!! And Mara, I'm sorry! But I couldn't take the rejection anymore. So I took the pages and tried to blame it on her."

"So where are the pages, Kathy?" Gerry asked. "How about you just give them back? Then we can sort this whole thing out."

Kathy looked down at Gerry, her expression wild like that of a caged animal. "No Gerry, that's not possible. I can't give them back because... because..." Her eyes darted back and forth as if searching for a reason. "Because I ate them!" she finally cried.

Gerry spat another mouthful of coffee.

"That's right," said Kathy. "I fucking ate

them. I eat vellum. I've been doing it for years! It's my dirty little secret. I started doing it ages ago, out of sheer desperation. I thought it might help me control my eating habits. That somehow the taste of that ancient calfskin would stop me from eating so many Reese's Peanut Butter Cups! But it didn't work. Nothing works! All it did was give me a new addiction. A taste for antique manuscripts!" Her eyes filled up with manic, junkie-like lust. "Oh, how I love them! The taste! The texture, Mm!"

Kathy leapt from the desk and ran to one side of the room, where several antique volumes were being temporarily stored on a shelf. She picked up the closest one, an Italian Renaissance era Bible, and began devouring the Book of Revelations. She ate the Four Horsemen, the Beast with seven heads, and the Whore of Babylon too. All were too confused to stop her.

"Oh, that's good," said Kathy, cramming pages in her mouth. "Ugh! Superb! I just love Italian!"

She dropped the book, twisted up her face, and let out a wail of inchoate madness.

"Oh, what am I doing?! I'm sick! Sick!

Behold, my shame!" she screamed, covering her face with her hands. "Now you all see me for what I am, a sexual predator! A liar! A book-eating freak! I no longer have any place amongst you. I belong in the ninth circle of Hell!"

Sobbing and screaming, Kathy ran for the nearest exit. No one tried to stop her, but they all followed after, if only to see what she'd do next. Thomas was first to rush after, his phone still filming. Mara followed the others in stunned silence.

They found Kathy on the roof overlooking the parking lot. She paced up and down, her makeup streaked with tears.

"It's time for my swan song," she wailed, teetering on the narrow ledge.

She pulled out her mobile phone and began swiping frantically. A moment later, a familiar guitar riff sounded from the phone's unusually loud speakers. The lyrics of Van Halen's "Jump" filled the tense air. Kathy put the phone down and started clapping her hands and dancing from side to side.

"Come on everyone," she said, "With me now!"

Employees watched in astonishment as Kathy danced with abandon on the ledge, careless of the deadly drop beside her and the unforgiving concrete below.

"Should we...call the police?" whispered someone. "An ambulance?"

"Call the guys in the fucking white coats," said another. "Call someone! Where's her husband?"

"Ten bucks says she trips before she can actually jump," Thomas said.

"Nah, she'll jump first," said Gerry.

The group kept watching, all too filled with secret sweet schadenfreude to do anything but stare. Kathy's dancing morphed into burlesque. She touched herself obscenely, unbuttoning her blouse and tearing it from her shoulders.

"I'm free. I'm free! Goodbye cruel world!" she called, struggling to kick off her pants. Turning to face the parking lot, she tripped on the garment round her ankles and flew, half-naked, toward the concrete below.

People gasped, then screamed in delayed horror.

"Stop!" someone shouted, far too late.

"Oh, fuck!" said another.

"She jumped!" said Gerry.

"No way. She totally tripped," said Thomas, who was still filming.

Gerry sighed and pulled out a crumpled ten from his pocket. Thomas took it without looking away from his phone.

The group slowly made their way over and peered from the ledge. Mara's eyes landed on what was left of Kathy, a stark smear of raspberry and glistening bone on gray pavement. A group of nearby school-children cried. Onlookers pulled out phones to document the scene. *A suicide? How exciting!* Mara could hear her coworkers buzzing and murmuring, the blipping of touch-screen buttons. Eventually someone got around to calling an ambulance.

Mara turned away, scarcely able to believe her own eyes. What the hell had just happened? Kathy had never sexually harassed her. Kathy hadn't eaten those stolen pages. Yet Mara had stood there and heard the same things as everyone else. She'd watched Kathy eat those Bible pages, confess to everything, then plunge to her death. How could Mara get so lucky?

She looked down into the parking lot one more time, wanting to remember the scene forever. From the roof Kathy looked like one of those smeared impressionist paintings she'd always been fawning over. "Oh, Mara isn't this Monet just gorgeous! Look at those flowers!"

Mara shook her head. "What the fuck happened, Kathy?" she muttered to herself.

A glint, like a single flickering flame, hooked her attention. It danced over the pink visceral mess down below. *No, it isn't. It can't be...*

Mara squinted, looking harder. She glimpsed Silfer hovering over the gore. He caught her eye, winked, and left just as quick as the wind.

Mara made her way downstairs and out into the grisly parking lot. All around her, people rushed to take photos before the paramedics showed up to scrape Kathy into a bag. There was screaming, crying, but Mara didn't notice or care. She was thinking about her devil.

Slamming shut the door to her apartment, Mara knew she had a stupid grin on her face. Kathy was dead. *Really* fucking dead. The problems, the fears that had been weighing on her shoulders, Silfer had swatted them away as if they'd been nothing more than pesky flies. Mara couldn't believe it. Never had she been so thankful for someone, demon or not.

There came a familiar-sounding *knock-knock-knock.* She opened the door and saw Silfer standing there, a ragged handful of flowers with weeping human faces gripped in his claws.

"Hey," he said. "Did you enjoy my surprise?"

Mara shook her head. "I... I can't even believe it. Oh, thank you!"

She forgot for a moment about the expanse between them, the fact he wasn't a solid form. She reached around to hug him, feeling only a space of warm, dry air.

"Damn it." She stepped back, looking at him. "Forgot about the whole touching thing. Want to come in?"

She moved aside, letting Silfer pass. Never had she wanted someone in her apartment so badly. He handed her the wilted humanesque flowers.

"Oh, uh, thanks, I'll just put these...."

Mara looked around, wondering where one should even put such nightmare flora. Water would only speed up decomposition, she imaged. In the end she put the bundle in the fridge, figuring she'd deal with it later. The flower heads squealed as she slammed the door. She had so many questions, things she wanted to say.

"You killed Kathy! Why would you do something like that?" she asked, still a little astonished at such a grand gesture as murder by demonic possession.

"Isn't it obvious, Mara?" he said. "I love you. I'd do anything for you."

Mara opened her mouth, closed it, taking in the full extent of his words. She felt that tight fist of cynicism and boredom she'd carried in the pit of her stomach for so long open, and finally release her. She could breathe for the first time in a long while.

"I..." she struggled to find the words. Words she'd always hated and avoided at all costs. Words used by poets and hippies to make fucking into something other than what it was. But she found at that moment

she wanted to say them more than anything.

"I love you so much it hurts. I want to
see you every day. I hate having all this
space between us. It's unbearable." She bit
her lip, not recognizing her own voice. What
was this demon doing to her?

Silfer looked at Mara, really looked at
her. The euphoria he felt was the sort of
sappy thing choirs of angels might sing
about, and yet, it was true. He smiled, staring into her eyes, seeing her love reflecting
back at him. An arrow of rapture pierced
his heart. Mara smiled back at him, radiant,
transfigured, more beautiful than ever. He
wanted to hold her so badly. His entire body
ached, even though he was only in spectral
form.

"Mara," he said. "Mara, I fucking love
you. I go to sleep thinking about you, wake
up thinking about you. I feel crazy wanting
to kiss you, hold you. More than anything,
I want to touch you. I want to be as close as
possible."

Instinctively he moved toward her,
wanting to brush her lips with his. But he
was only an infernal ghost. A shadow filled

with dim heat.

Usually when Mara heard words like that, saw her date coming at her, trying to kiss her, she made a silent note to herself not to answer the phone next time he called. Yet this time was different; for once she wanted a guy just as bad as he wanted her.

"Me too, as close as possible. I want to crawl inside you and live next to your heart." She gushed, unable to stop herself. "It makes my chest ache wanting to see you. I constantly want to be with you, morning and night. Sleeping beside you, smelling your skin, feeling your weight on me. I want your hands running over my ribs. Fuck I can't believe how much I love you..."

Mirroring his movements, she leaned in closer. Her kiss met with a brush of warm desire and emptiness. Mara couldn't believe it. For once she liked a guy, *loved* a guy, and yet she couldn't even touch him.

"Shit, really?" she said, seeing the same look of irritation and longing on his face.

"We can't touch," he said. "Not until you die and incarnate in Hell. Until then, there's only words, sights, sounds..." he gazed at her, a look of raw hunger on his wicked face. "Mara, let me see you. Even just to see you…"

Given the choice of either dying or taking off her clothes for momentary pleasure, Mara took the easier of the two paths. "Okay. Sure." She'd been asked to do stranger things in her time. She pulled off her shirt and kicked her pants off. She stood there in mismatched faded black underwear she'd bought from the Good Will for a dollar fifty.

Silfer shuddered with desire. Her body was slender, pale, beautiful. But most of all, her essence, truly and completely, simply *Her*, drew him in. The most delicious thing in the entire universe. Down in Hell his sex grew painfully hard, a state reflected in his spectral form as his hard-on stabbed at his pants. A blunt bayonet trying to puncture the side of a black canvas tent. "Mara, fuck, you're beautiful," he said.

Mara didn't know how to respond. She hated comments directed at her personal appearance. She avoided words like *sexy* or *beautiful* at all costs. When she did hear them, she usually thought they were unimaginative bullshit used to get into her pants. But here, he couldn't get into her pants, only look and watch. Mara liked that. She decided *What the hell*? She'd play this game.

Looking at Silfer, Mara slid her hand down the front of her faded panties.

"How's this? Is this what you want to see?" she asked, slipping a finger into her cunt, watching him watching her.

"Oh yes," he said, taking in a sharp breath. Instinctively his hand went to his prick, squeezing it through his pants, wishing it was her hand, not his. "Yeah, tell me what you want."

A half smile sat softy on her lips. "I want to run my tongue down your sternum, over your stomach. Lower and lower, until I'm between your legs. Kiss every tender spot I can find. Slide my mouth down the shaft of your cock. Encircle the tender head with the tip of my tongue. Bring you into my mouth slow, deep. I want to savor every inch of you for as long as possible until you cum inside my mouth. Then I'll swallow you down into my guts. I want to climb on top of you and press you inside me. Crush you down into the bed and fuck you until your eyes roll back in your head and you beg no more, no more."

"Oh, fuck, yes. You're incredible...Show me..." he trailed off, watching her push her panties down and drop to her knees.

Mara liked this game. She was slick when she slipped in a second and third finger. Her eyes remained on him while she thrust them in and out of her aching sex. Her wrist massaged her clit as she moved her fingers slowly, evenly. Wanting pleasure for herself, but wanting to give it to him even more. She sighed, ragged with longing.

Silfer's breath grew harsher, as urgent as her own. On her knees, her head was at the same height as his crotch. Her eyes were fixed on his, radiating hunger and lust. He didn't know what he wanted more – to slip his cock between her lips, sink himself deep into her cunt, or simply to kiss her. In truth he wanted it all, and more still. Watching her like this was almost a torment for the damned, like the fate of old Tantalus.

"Mara," he said, slipping a hand down his pants. "I want whatever you desire. Ride me as hard as you can. When you get tired, we can switch positions. You on your back, or on all fours. I can hold your hips and thrust in. Then with my cock deep inside you, throbbing, both of us aching for motion, for friction, just holding it off..."

"Please I just want you.... fuck me... God I'm so fucking slick, why did you stop? You're so cruel..." Mara gasped, continuing to fuck herself. Her words mixed with moans and laughter. Watching him, she ached for his hands to touch her, explore all the lines and bends of her body. She wanted to feel him on her, his thickness inside of her, filling her up so much more than her fingers.

As she felt herself falling into orgasm, her pleasure completely unfolded within her. She leaned forward, holding herself up with her trembling free hand. Plunging her fingers in deeper. His name hovering on the tip of her tongue. She thought about *his tongue*. How she wanted it to find hers. She hungered to feel his teeth on her skin, biting down, making her bleed as she finished. Her entire being aching for him. Wanting him to lick, taste her mouth, her blood, her cunt. Absorb the lust she had for him.

"Mara," he whispered, gazing down

at her, so close to him yet so impossibly far. He could feel her raw craving, her desire to be touched, to be fucked. "I... want to suck on your beautiful blood, drink you in. I want you to feel the stinging pain, the absolute pleasure of my cock deep in you. Your blood and my cum." Silfer's whole being was a blaze of longing. He couldn't just stand there and watch anymore.

"*Please*...I want all that." Mara gasped.

Silfer ripped off his coat of lost souls and stood naked before her, his tail sticking up from behind, his prick throbbing with painful need. He grabbed the shaft and began. Glancing from Mara's face to her cunt, how he longed to kiss her, thrust himself between her thighs. *Her cunt, her cunt, her cunt...* Oh, how he wanted it enfolding him, gripping him, taking all of him in. Carrying him to the brink of inevitable euphoria. To plunge deep inside it, hold himself there. Rutting like a beast until he felt her quivering around him, impaled by his sex.

Mara... her name was like a mantra in his mind as the pleasure exploded in flashes within him. Her name came out in a breathless whisper. His cum passed through her flesh with spectral weightlessness, hitting the floor beneath her, bubbling and smoking with hellish heat.

Mara, breathless, rolled onto her back, stared up at the crack in her ceiling, the room spinning around her. She let her aching legs relax and fall open.

"Fuck, I love you," she said, waiting for Silfer to say it back. When he remained silent, she looked at him, following his intense gaze down to her inner thigh. "What?" She looked down at her leg. "That? It's just a birthmark or something, it's gross." She closed her legs, suddenly feeling self-conscious. She sat up and pulled on her underwear. Silfer continued staring at her leg. Mara just wanted to find her pants.

"Oh fuck," whispered Silfer. The mark on her thigh looked eerily like 777. "Mara, are you sure that's a birthmark? Not a tattoo?"

"I think I'd remember if I'd got a tattoo. I'm not that much of a mess. Why? Do you hate girls with tattoos or something?" Mara looked at him, feeling slightly irritated. Why was this a thing? "It's just a birthmark. I've been thinking about getting it lasered off, though. It's not a big deal. Just don't look at it." Mara pulled her pants on. The story of her life, hot sex followed by an awkward conversation.

"No, Mara, you don't understand," he said. "Just... Fuck!" He stood up, pacing, running his hands through his hair. "It'll be okay," he muttered, more to himself than to her. "It's okay. Maybe it's just a coincidence. I just... I better check the book just to be sure."

"Book?" Mara lit a cigarette and sat back down on the floor, confused and concerned.

Silfer took a deep breath, summoning a large leather book in a mess of smoke and fire. *The Book of the Elect* contained the names of all the souls who were chosen. He paused for a moment, filled with apprehension. Finally flipping the tome open, he searched for Mara's name. His finger paused on the sharp black letters. His guts twisted when he read her name. He felt their future together – the future he longed for – being torn from his grasp just like that.

"Fuck!" he said, tossing the book across the room. It hit the wall and vanished in a hail of sparks.

Mara meanwhile got up and opened the fridge for something to eat, only to find the weeping flower heads. She closed the fridge, thinking she'd eat later. She watched Silfer pace back and forth across the floor.

"What?" she finally asked.

Silfer stared at her, still overcome with longing and love, despite it all.

Mara didn't like the look on his face. "Just tell me. What? Am I dying or something?" When he failed to crack a smile, Mara knew it was going to be bad.

Silfer swallowed the lump that had developed in his throat. Why did the universe have to be so cruel?!

"Mara, that birthmark," he began, trying to steady his voice. "It's a brand, put there by God. It marks you as one of his chosen. I checked the book, to make sure, and... well, you're one of the Elect, Mara. You're going to Heaven. Even if you murder babies and join a human trafficking ring, you'll still end up with the angels."

Mara let the words sink in.

"No, that's not possible. It's just a stupid birthmark." Her voice trailed off as she thought about the small twisted thing on her skin. She looked up at Silfer, who stood silently before her. "I don't want to go to Heaven. That would mean..." She shook her head, realizing the weight his words carried. If there was no way for her to get into Hell, how would they ever be together? After today with Kathy, then the sex, the love she felt gnawing at her heart... the idea felt unfathomable. It made her angry. "Fuck, I don't want to spend all eternity with some asshole angels. That one guy was enough. There has to be something we can do!"

Silfer put a hand to his mouth. His breathing came heavy, filled with emotion. He couldn't be without her, especially not now. How badly he wanted to reach out for her. He settled for stepping closer, as close as he could without his intangible form overlapping with hers.

"You're right," he said. "There has to be a way. I won't be apart from you. Mara, I love you. I've always hated everyone, but I love you. Even if I have to rip off Gabriel's wings and poke out Azrael's eyes, I'll find a way for us to be together."

Brain Removal Device

SILFER LOOKED UP at the edifice before him and scowled. Libraries in Hell used to be imposing, majestic things, designed in the style of Gothic churches or Greco-Roman temples. He remembered visiting them as a child, staring up in awe at the ancient friezes of triumphant devils raping angels in every conceivable orifice, a glorious vision of the End of Days showing devil-kind triumphant.

Things had changed since then. They'd knocked the old libraries down or turned them into expensive apartment blocks for yuppie devils. The Third Circle's new library, AKA the Ed Gein Library, named after one of the most amusing mortals of the

Twentieth Century, was a modern abomination straight from the fetid anti-imagination of a Damien Hirst try-hard.

Made up of arbitrary arrangements of interlocking square blocks and panels, the building looked like a Rubik's Cube pulled apart by an angry child. Most of the panels were thick glass. Pressed against them were truncated, bisected, vivisected, or otherwise mutilated souls. All were displayed in cross-sections, like exhibits at an anatomy museum. Except they were all still animate and squirming. This way visitors could enjoy the raw organs palpitating up against the glass.

Other panels were opaque, like obsidian, filled with captive souls that would bump against the glass like fish in an aquarium, silently screaming. Yet not all the ghosts lived in eternal torment. One of them obviously had a sense of humor about his plight. He would regularly fly up to the barrier, bend over, and press his cock and balls against the gleaming surface. Still, as funny as that ghost was, it wasn't enough to dampen Silfer's disgust towards the building overall. He made his way to the entrance, glancing at the tacky Koons-like sculptures of red cartoon devils flanking the entrance.

Silfer's revulsion only deepened as he stepped inside. Libraries in Hell were once quiet places, patrolled by matronly devil lady librarians who'd flay anyone if they heard so much as a whisper. But libraries weren't for quiet reading anymore. They were "learning hubs" or "information centers" where "the demonic community could congregate and share knowledge." Or at least, that was the idea.

In practical terms, it just meant they'd removed a lot of books to make way for computers and comfy couches. The computers were almost exclusively used for looking at pornography or carrying out extra-marital sexting. A quick glance into the library's principal room showed at least ten devils, male and female, blatantly pleasuring themselves to images downloaded off the Hell-net. Among the clusters of tables and couches sprawled scores of student devils eating potato chips, watching HellTube videos, and chatting to each other loudly. A bookish devil in the corner tried to hush them, but was told to go somewhere else if he wanted to read.

Silfer ignored them all and headed for the part of the library that still had the actual books in it. It was quieter, but still noisy. Hipster library workers had replaced the matronly devil ladies. They strolled around putting books on shelves in seemingly random arrangements whilst listening to shitty music on their iPods. Silfer put on his own iPod and listened to Excruciate Rex. As he listened to the songs he'd heard with Mara by his side, his heart filled with sweet and painful longing, and he remembered again why he'd come to the library.

He decided to start by researching the mechanics of salvation and damnation. The books in that section were ancient, bound in human flesh. Silfer sat down on the floor in front of the shelf and began flipping through volumes. He looked through all the classic tomes, from *Predestination: Divine Sovereignty & You*, to *The Secret History of God & His Elect,* down to the classic *From Ancient to Modern times: Reflections on the Chosen, the Damned, and Everything Else.* Growing desperate, Silfer even tried a few more modern ones, suck as *I Thought I*

Was God's Chosen One? and *Are You There God? Please Leave Me Alone.*

After a few hours he sighed and stood up to crack his back.

"Nothing," he whispered. "Fucking nothing."

Maybe just browsing the stacks wasn't the best way to go? There were a lot of things hidden away in archive rooms, sequestered in special collections, or just plain lost by inept librarians.

He went to the nearest computer and began searching the catalogue, starting out with the most basic search terms. "The Elect," "Salvation," "Divine Birthmarks," etc. He hit the enter key, a yellowed human tooth, and watched the results come up.

"What the fuck?" he whispered.

The catalogue entries were confusing and horribly written. No doubt perpetrated by the same iPod-sporting hipster devils currently strutting around putting books on the wrong shelves. Still, there were a couple of volumes that looked promising, even if the details on their contents were vague. The most promising one of all, *Hanströnem's Handbook,* was to be found in the rare collections department.

Silfer made a digital request for the book and headed over to the departmental desk. It was a relatively quiet section of the library with large empty tables. The collection itself was locked away behind thick tempered glass. The air smelled musty. It reminded him of the museum where he'd first seen Mara.

Mara, he thought. Again he felt that bittersweet longing. Thoughts of her turned into fantasies, simple at first, the two of them holding hands, walking along the beach of the river Styx. Then more and more lurid, her ass in the air, her eyes full of lust, her glistening slit in his face.

"Silfer Incinerator?"

Silfer looked up at the hipster devil librarian standing before him, holding a human soul on a leash. The woman wore nothing but a dog collar. Someone had tattooed her body with spidery handwriting.

"What is this?" said Silfer, nodding towards her.

"This is *Hanströnem's Handbook*, said the librarian. "It's in a new format – a living book. You can read her, or she can recite the book's contents out loud."

Silfer sighed as he looked at the tattooed woman/book.

"This is fucking dumber then Kindle," he whispered.

He took the leash nonetheless, pulled the woman over to the table, and laid her out. The volume was scanty, hence how it could be inked onto a single human body. Of course, it wasn't very convenient to read. The text on her eyelids was difficult to make out. As was the text in the crack of her ass and that on her labia. Still, he persisted until he'd read her from tits to toes.

"Fuck," he said.

Still no new knowledge. He was slipping into despair, wondering if it was even possible to liberate Mara from her damned heavenly destiny. And even if he did, what then? Would she be ready to die and come to Hell? Or would she want to wait to die by accident or illness? What would they do in the interim? Loving someone so much, yet being unable to touch them, it was almost unbearable. He burned for her, like the Pits of the Duat. Surely there was a way they could consummate their love in the flesh, even while being trapped on separate planes of existence.

A black light bulb flashed in his head. "Fucking of course!"

Feeling overjoyed, he kissed the living book on the cheek, then ran from the library to see his beloved, if not in his own flesh, then perhaps in someone else's.

Mara stared out the window. The day was bright and cheery, but inside she felt dark and miserable. "Fucking universe," she muttered, flicking ash outside, watching the gentle summer breeze carry it away. For a moment she thought about throwing herself out, plunging to her death. Suicides were supposed to go to Hell. Mara was curious to see what would happen. She leaned forward and looked out. She lived on the third floor. Knowing her luck, she'd probably just end up paralyzed.

She heard knocking on her door, but ignored it. Probably just someone from work, coming by to cry about Kathy. Mara didn't want to hear about it anymore. She wondered if Kathy was in Hell. But what did it matter? Mara *wasn't*. No, she was stuck here until she died. Then on to that gated community of paranoid white people and shitty music in the sky. She couldn't believe this was happening to her. The knocking continued.

"Fine! Fine, what is it?" she yelled. "Christ, I'm coming!"

Silfer stood in the hall, looking annoyingly cheerful. Mara figured he'd probably come to break up with her. What good was a girlfriend if you couldn't touch her?

"Hey," she said, waiting for the inevitable.

"Hey," he said, stepping inside, drawing close to her, whispering, his voice almost trembling. "I've missed you so much, my love."

Mara shrugged. "Hm."

She turned and wandered from the open door, not in the mood. Even seeing him was depressing. Whatever he had to say, she didn't want to hear it right now.

"Mara, I've been researching our problem," he said, following her. "You know, trying to find ways to stop you going to Heaven. Unfortunately, I haven't found anything... yet. But there is a way for us to be together! Well, sort of. At least temporarily, for a couple of hours. You might think it's kinda weird though."

Mara sat at her kitchen table, listening to him go on. He seemed so enthusiastic, so optimistic. Normally that sort of thing would make Mara sick, but the idea of a couple of hours together sounded better than nothing. She looked at her devil. He really was trying, despite the difficulty of the situation. His dedication touched her; it made her want to try too.

"Weird, huh?" she said. "I guess I could do weird for you."

"Okay," said Silfer with a smile. "Meet me outside in half an hour, and we'll go look for something suitable together!"

Mara and Silfer wandered through the park and sat down on a bench. In the late day sun there were plenty of people to choose from.

"So just anyone?" Mara asked, looking around. People were playing Frisbee. Another man was walking his dog. A couple lounged under shady trees. They all looked annoying. Mara would never want to fuck any of them.

"Almost anyone," Silfer said. "They have to have a mental vulnerability though. So crazy people are ideal. Crazy people, junkies, those with a weak mind, the mentally retarded..."

"Wow. Sounds like a bunch of winners. However will I choose?" Mara rolled her eyes. To her left, a homeless man was gathering cans from the trash. His clothes were filthy. He was unshaven. Mara liked his damaged, filmy white eye. "Oh, what about him?" she asked.

Silfer peered at the man, eyeing the cracks in his soul. "Actually, he would work. But would you seriously want me to possess a guy like that? He's pretty gross. I'd have to take him to the barber, give him a shower, a shave, it'd take ages. And who knows what diseases –"

"No, I'm sure it's fine." Mara wasn't looking at his clothes, his unshaven skin, but at that one glistening white eye. It reminded her of a shiny marble. It was hard to find a man with just one cloudy eye. "Just try it," she urged him.

Silfer shrugged. "Okay. Whatever you want, my love." He strode over to the can-collecting hobo. *This is the weird part*, he thought. Still, there was no time to waste. Back in Hell the Belphegor Candle was burning!

He stepped into the hobo's body, pushing the man's soul aside. For a moment he brushed against it, as one might brush against dusty cobwebs in a filthy old house. He felt a crawling, itching sensation. Inchoate screams of madness echoed from the man's soul in a chorus of fractured voices. Silfer pushed the humanity down as though he were stuffing clothes into a cheap suitcase, until the hobo's psyche was trapped in the innermost recesses of the hijacked flesh.

Having claimed the body, Silfer opened the hobo's one good eye and stared at the world. He inhaled through the hobo's nostrils, smelling the filth caking the meat suit. Layers of soiled clothing cocooned the scuzzy skin. His ass crack felt foul, as though the cleft of his buttocks were a bread roll smeared with peanut butter. Silfer didn't want to know what was down there.

His crotch felt like it was swimming in filth. Who knew how much dick cheese was under that unwashed foreskin?

Maybe this wasn't such a good idea, he thought. Then he saw Mara, beautiful Mara, smiling at him. He strode over to her with the hobo's creaking legs. If he could only hold her hand – just touch her fingers, brush her cheek – then this would all be worthwhile.

He drew closer, wild with excitement at the prospect of finally being able to touch her. His raw desire filled the stolen blood bag with inhuman delight. The hobo's heart began racing, thumping, pounding, moving in a frenzied staccato beat. Pain radiated through his chest, along with a sickening constriction. He clutched at the mortal's heart.

Mara watched the possessed man fall and land just inches from her feet. His head bounced off the sidewalk with a sickening *clunk!* She didn't know what had happened. Soon people were running over, yelling for someone to get help. Mara watched a woman turn the man over and take his pulse. "I think he's had a heart attack," she said, to no one in particular. Silfer stood above a corpse. The man was dead, slain by the heat of the devil's unholy love.

He sighed and sat down next to Mara. "Well, that didn't work," he said.

"What happened?"

"Well, my desire for you is pretty intense. So when I took over that guy's body, his heart couldn't take the strain. I guess it's not just any mortal that can be a vessel for infernal lust. Which means we need to find someone weak of mind, but strong in body."

The pair left the crowd and headed downtown, hoping for more options. Mara stopped in front of the gym. The idea made her gag, but it was the only place she could think of that had strong bodies and weak minds.

"What about in there?"

She pointed through the window. Inside, a man was screaming at a woman to run faster on a treadmill. He blew a whistle in her face. The sweating woman jumped off and ran over to a bike and started cycling. The man followed, hurling insults, asking if she wanted to be fat forever.

What an asshole, Mara thought. "Can

you possess that guy?" she asked. The thought of tying that man down and gagging him, just shutting him up, was enough for her to overlook how repulsed she was by him.

Silfer peered at the personal trainer. The crack in the guy's soul was massive. A perfect piece of split wood. Plus the guy looked healthy as a horse, with bulging muscles and rock-hard abs. He obviously did plenty of weights. Probably loads of cardio too. If anyone could withstand being a vessel for Silfer's otherworldly desire, it was probably him. "Okay, let's give it a shot," he said.

Silfer stepped through the glass wall of the gym and made a bee-line for the trainer. He possessed him the same way he'd possessed the hobo, by stepping into his flesh and pushing his soul aside. Silfer felt the world through the man's stolen senses and smiled; this body was indeed very strong. It didn't smell like piss or have shit caked in its ass crack either, which was a definite plus.

Silfer turned to the trainer's client, who was huffing away on a stationary bike. "You've done a magnificent job today, honey," he said. "Why don't you finish up now and celebrate with a tasty doughnut?"

The woman stopped cycling, her eyes wide with joy. "A doughnut?" she said. "Really?!" But Silfer was already walking away, heading towards Mara. He could see her through the window. So beautiful, so wonderful. His stolen heart hammered like a black metal double-bass drum, but thankfully there were no signs of an impending heart attack.

This is it, he thought. *We're going to be together!*

He raced to the door, beaming with happiness. And yet, as he hurried, he noticed something disturbing about this stolen body; it seemed to lack weight in the groin area. Silfer stepped outside, then opened the man's gym shorts and looked inside.

"Oh, fuck no. Really guy?"

The man was hung like a five-year-old. Years of steroid abuse had shrunken his tackle to a prepubescent state. Silfer couldn't fuck Mara with this!

"Motherfucker!" he said.

In a fit of pique, Silfer walked the body off the curb and directly under a passing truck.

The horn blared; bystanders screamed. Mara turned and walked the other way, avoiding the splash of blood on the pavement. She crossed the street. On the other side, Silfer appeared beside her.

"So I guess he's a no?" she asked.

Silfer reiterated the problem in the guy's pants.

"Figures," Mara muttered, feeling more frustrated than ever.

The pair crossed to a playground and sat down on the edge of a fountain, watching parents hovering behind their children like flies over rot. For a moment, Mara considered a father standing beside the swing set. Then his boyfriend came up and kissed him. No, Mara would feel weird forcing her cunt on a man who liked cock. Besides, he looked too well adjusted and happy; his soul probably didn't have enough cracks in it.

"What are we going to do?" she said. "This is harder than I thought."

Silfer shrugged, feeling her frustration.

Mara observed a young man lying on a bench to her left. He wasn't filthy, but he definitely wasn't well-groomed either.

He stared at clouds, completely in his own world. A child ran past him. He turned and smiled, looking dazed. His arm dangled off the bench. Mara noticed track marks along the inside of his forearm.

"What about a junkie?" she asked, turning to Silfer. Both looked at the man. "I mean, he doesn't look too high right now. And he's younger than me, I'm sure his heart is fine. He can't be too far gone."

Silfer saw the guy had so many cracks in his soul he looked like porcelain that'd had the shit kicked out of it by an especially belligerent child.

"Easy," he said. "We'll just have to be careful of diseases."

He walked over to the man. Not wasting any time, he went through the increasingly familiar procedure of possessing a human body. A moment later he sat up on the bench, clothed in stolen flesh, seeing through stolen eyes. A wave of euphoria washed over him. He stood, stepped towards Mara, then stumbled.

His body felt... *odd*. The bones were hollow, like bird bones. The skin as light as crinkled-up wrapping paper. Yet, he also felt heavy somehow. There were stones in his guts, surrounded by aroused snakes all writhing together. He took another step, then almost fell over. Suddenly the hollow bones weren't so light.

Silfer stumbled to his knees. The pavement was scintillating. No, not scintillating, *crawling*. Thousands of asphalt maggots were writhing from the skin of the earth, born from some fathomless corruption. The sun was spilling into the horizon like an egg yolk into a pan. The light was thick, viscous. He could probably drink it. Perhaps it would drown him, choke him, fill all his pores, until he too was a part of that egg-yellow sun. Food for some bellowing god.

But he didn't want to be food for a god. He wanted something else... That's right, Mara! His only love. He glanced around, trying to find her amidst the crawling sidewalk and the hideous humanoid creatures that cavorted and jeered all around him. *Ignore them*, he thought, fighting off the panic as wild midgets screamed murder songs just a few feet from his naked antennae. *Just find Mara.*

There she was! A goddess, naked and beautiful. Standing among the shimmering mist of a waterfall. She reached out toward him, bosom bare, cunt wet and inviting. He ran to her, ignoring the stones and snakes in his belly. Soon he was under the waterfall with her, bathing his crotch in her soaking gash, slipping his arms around her strangely unyielding form. Her lips were hard and uninviting, but still she was beautiful. Slowly she began to yield to him, and him to her, as he took on her semblance of immovable metal.

"Mara," he moaned. "Mara, you are my everything!"

He sighed with delight. Finally, oh finally, they were together!

Mara stood off to the left, unsure if she should say anything or not. Unsure what was even going on. "Uh... is everything alright?" Silfer was so entranced with the carved cherub in the middle of the fountain he didn't seem to hear her. She wondered if maybe that junkie had taken something.

Fuck!

Mara waded out into the shallow water, trying to get Silfer's attention, attempting to unwrap his arms from around the stone statue.

"That's not me. Hey!" She slapped him. "You need to leave that body. This guy is obviously on something. This is no good." She shook him, but Silfer kept running his hands up and down the figure, murmuring into its unhearing ear. "Can you hear me in there?" Mara knocked on his head with a fist. "Get out of there. He's higher than a fucking kite."

Silfer didn't hear her at first. He was too busy tasting the juice of the disintegrating universe on his three-fold cosmic tongue. The water flowed into his body, his body into the water, a gateway to universal oneness. His pores were opening, his body dissolving into the infinite churning miasma of earth and sky, filled with asphalt maggots, egg-yolk sun, the cloying breath of automobiles. Who was Silfer anyway?

"Silfer fucking snap out of it!"

The blow hit him hard across the temple. The voice pierced his being. Mara's voice, wonderful Mara. Of course he would obey her. Of course! He stepped out of the skin-suit and found that the waterfall was merely a fountain, filled with quarters and spattered with pigeon shit. The "Mara" he'd been embracing was a chubby cherub pissing water. The real Mara was slapping the druggie. Concerned citizens approached from nearby, alarmed by the sight of a woman with a shaved head accosting a drug addict in the waters of a public park.

"Mara," said Silfer, trying to draw her attention. "I'm back. Let's get the fuck out of here!"

Silfer and Mara trudged back towards Mara's apartment, their spirits lower than the sun sinking in the sky.

"Well, that was a waste of time," Mara said.

The pair turned the corner and walked in silence, both lost in thought as to what to do next. The idea had sounded so easy. Too bad people were so stupid.

"Mara! Mara! *Hell*-o!"

Mara knew that voice – Cara. She hadn't thought about Todd and Cara since her dream. Last time she'd seen them, Todd's revolver had been pressed to Cara's head.

Mara had trouble looking at the couple standing out in their yard, still very much alive. The dream had been so real. She could still see the manic look in Todd's eye, the mascara running down Cara's face as she realized she was going to die.

"Damn it," Mara muttered, stopping and forcing a half smile. "Hey, didn't see you guys there." They were hacking at shrubs and over watering half-dead flowers.

"How are you? What have you been up to?" said Cara as she set down her pruning shears and walked over, putting her arm around Todd, who leaned casually against the fence.

Mara sighed. "Well, I saw two guys die today. Then a junkie went crazy near the playground and started trying to fuck a statue in the fountain. It was hilarious."

Todd and Cara looked at one another, then back at Mara before they burst out laughing. "Oh, Mara! You're *so* funny! Isn't she *so* funny, honey?" Cara asked Todd.

Todd nodded and gave an artificial smile. "So funny. Ha-ha." He slapped Cara's ass, making her jump. Both began laughing all over again.

"Well, I've got to get home." Mara turned and scurried away, Silfer at her side. They left Todd and Cara giggling on the lawn.

"I fucking hate them," hissed Mara as they stepped out of earshot. "Did you see what they were doing to those shrubs? Why buy such big shrubs and plant them next to the house, only to hack them down to half their size? Just buy smaller shrubs!"

Her comment was met with silence.

"Silfer?"

She turned, looking up and down the street, but he was gone. Mara didn't blame him; not even a demon could stand talking to Cara and Todd.

"Fuck!"

Silfer was back in his apartment in Hell. The Belphegor Candle – the expensive and highly illegal magickal tool he'd used to travel to Earth and possess human bodies – had finally burned out, sucking him back to his own dimension. Talk about awful timing. He'd just found the perfect candidate for possession!

I've got to go buy another candle, he thought. The purchase would cripple his bank account, but he didn't really care. As he sat on his bed he smiled, even though the neighbors on his right were loudly torturing a sex slave, and the ones on the left were watching "Who Wants to Skull-Fuck a Millionaire" on maximum volume. Still, he couldn't help but be happy. For soon, very soon, he'd be in Mara's arms.

Silfer lit the Belphegor Candle and lay back in the magickal circle he'd inscribed on the floor. With a familiar sensation his soul tore loose from his body and rocketed up towards earth. Intangible, he passed through the floor of his apartment building, through couches and giant cockroaches, then up into Hell's fiery skies where scarlet-feathered vultures cut through the sulphureous clouds.

Piercing the mystical membrane between the dimensions, he moved into earth's molten core, then up through fathomless layers of rock and underground oceans of oil. Through fossils and Indian bones. Through the corpse of some guy who'd probably been murdered by the mob. Through sewer pipes and electrical cables. Squeezing past a top layer of rebar and concrete, he finally found himself standing in a large home improvement store, staring at his chosen prey.

There was Todd, Mara's vapid neighbor, standing with his wife Cara beside a vast wall of paint swatches. Cara was wearing gym clothes even though she wasn't at the gym. Todd's outfit was so awful Silfer had second thoughts about possessing the guy. He wore a beige polo and puce trousers. *Puce? Fucking seriously?* The trousers were ridiculously tight and somewhat short, making them look as if they'd shrunk in the wash. He wore shit-brown loafers without socks. Or maybe he was wearing those short socks that hide beneath the rim of the shoe. Silfer couldn't tell and didn't care. The net result was Todd seemed very keen to show off his bare manly ankles.

Silfer didn't get this new human fashion at all. Sure, it might work for a submissive twink, loudly advertising how much he wanted to get blasted in the ass. But for a presumably straight guy like Todd, it seemed to send all the wrong signals.

Cara and Todd flipped through the paint swatches. Silfer didn't care if they were flipping through leathery labias at Ed Gein's house. He was only here for one thing – Todd's body. Or, as Silfer preferred to think of it, Todd's transferable meat machine.

Silfer, taking one last look at Todd, decided it was now or never. He climbed into the man dressed as a boy, as though he were entering a tiny, uncomfortable car.

Todd flinched. His soul instinctively fought for dominion, but resistance was futile. His soul was fractured, his willpower weak. Here was a guy who wore puce trousers for fuck's sake. He didn't have a chance against a devil from Hell. Within moments Silfer asserted control, stamping Todd's soul into the innermost recesses of his flesh.

Silfer looked out through Todd's blue eyes at Todd's WASPish wife.

"What do you think of these?" asked Cara as she showed him what looked like a series of utterly identical pale white swatches. "I can't decide between Antique Parchment, Elephant Ivory, or Southern Cotton.

Or maybe this Alabaster Skin? They're all so calming. I think they'll open the space right up. I just don't want whatever we choose to clash with the dove gray paint on the statement wall. You know? Todd?" Cara looked up at her husband. "Are you even listening?"

"They're all fucking awful," said Silfer. "But I don't give a shit. Pick whatever. I'm outta here."

Cara's face went blank with shock as Silfer turned and strode away, whistling a song by Excruciate Rex, the first one he and Mara had listened to together. He chuckled to himself. The look on Cara's face!

Then he heard her squeaky gym shoes coming after him.

"Todd!" she said, rushing in front of him and cutting off his exit. "What on earth has gotten into you! Where are you going?"

"I've got stuff to do, okay?" he said. "I don't have time for this fuckery."

"But... but this is our day!" said Cara, dumbfounded. "We planned it! We're going to pick the colors for the family room. Then choose the fabric for new drapes. You promised we could have lunch at The Olive

Garden! Then Mark and Linda wanted us to come over for drinks, and watch that funny dating show you love. Todd?"

Silfer cringed, imaging Todd's life. If anything, he was doing this guy a big favor.

"I'm not doing any of that shit," said Silfer. "Pick whatever stupid paint and hideous curtains you want. Then you can eat Linda's pussy while Mark fucks you up the ass. Whatever. Have a good time!"

He pushed past her, hoping this was the end. But it wasn't.

Cara grabbed the sleeve of Todd's beige shirt. "Todd, how dare you talk to me like that!" she hissed, so the other customers couldn't hear. "Why are you doing this? Is this about what happened with me and Stewart again? Because I thought we covered all that in therapy. You need to let it go, Todd. We were in Florida, for Christ's sake! People get loose down there, anything goes. Now come back and help me pick these colors!"

She tugged at his arm. Silfer tried to pull away. Cara dug her fingernails into his flesh. He sighed and let her drag Todd's body back towards the swatches as though he were an errant child.

I guess we have to do this the hard way.

Silfer looked around, spotted a display of framing hammers on a nearby shelf. A single clipped blow punched the claw through her temple, into her parietal lobe. Silfer watched Cara drop without emotion. Blood trickled out onto the store's concrete floor.

"Now that's a nice colour for the feature wall," he said, even though no one was listening. These home improvement stores were so fucking massive a person could probably hide a Sherman tank inside of one, or host a full-blown orgy among the carpet samples without anyone noticing.

Whistling the Hellish tune, he dragged Cara's twitching body into a nearby aisle and covered up the corpse with a stray piece of AstroTurf. There was still a red stain on the floor he should deal with, but his time was limited. The Belphegor Candle was burning. He was pretty sure the place had security cameras, but couldn't will himself to care. He had more pressing needs concerning Mara and a bed.

Mara stepped into her bedroom and saw someone sitting in the shadows.

"What the fuck?" she said, recoiling. "Todd?"

Mara stared at the man. It was definitely her neighbor. But he'd shaved his head, and the smirk he usually wore was missing. "Todd! What are you doing here?"

"Not Todd," he said, getting up. "It's me, Silfer. I took Todd's body."

"But... but I thought we were going to give up on that?"

"I know," he said. "But just before I had to leave, I saw your neighbor, and I knew he was perfect. Weak mind, strong body. He's the ideal vessel."

"I guess," said Mara. "But seriously, Todd? I mean, ugh! He's awful."

"What's so wrong with him? Obviously spends a lot of time at the gym." Silfer poked Todd's tanned, rock hard midsection. "He's got great core strength."

"Yeah, maybe, but his clothes..."

"The clothes can come off," he said.

Silfer kicked off the over-priced sweatshop loafers, tore off the polo and the puce pants. Todd's stolen vessel stood naked before Mara. She examined him. The body of a complete moron, with her true love's spirit inside. She couldn't help but laugh.

"What?" he said.

"I was just thinking Todd's always been a tool. Now he's literally a tool of your will."

Silfer smiled and stepped towards her. Mara couldn't help but flinch a little.

"What's wrong?" he asked, noticing her reaction.

"It's just so weird," she said. "I can't stand Todd."

"Don't think of this body as Todd's," he said. "Right now, it's mine. I'm the one inside it. I'm the one who'll be touching you, feeling you. Mara, I want to *taste* you. I want all of you."

Mara peered at him and chewed her lip. He had a point. It wasn't Todd. That much was obvious when he spoke and used words with more than one syllable. Plus, he wasn't a junkie or a dead homeless man. He looked better with his hair shaved and no clothes on. She shut her eyes for a moment. *It's not Todd, it's not Todd*, she repeated to herself. It was her lover, cloaked in Todd's skin. She liked that idea. Mara decided *fuck it*, she would make Todd's body her whore.

Without a word she slipped off her clothes, let Silfer draw her in close against the stolen body.

Silfer wrapped his arm around Mara. Beautiful, fascinating Mara. Not sweet, but deliciously bitter. The companion of his soul. The one he'd been waiting a lifetime to encounter.

For a second Mara fought back the urge to cringe as she felt Todd's arm wrap around her. His arms were unusually smooth for those of a man. He probably shaved, or knowing him, waxed every inch of his body. Or made Cara do it. Mara tried to put the image out of her mind. She couldn't think about Todd and Cara's joint grooming session if she wanted to enjoy this.

Silfer ran his fingers down the smooth skin of her shoulder, feeling the small of her back, the tight curve of her ass. She was pale, lean, almost bony, but her body felt strong and warm. Mara kissed him first, pressing herself close, her heat melting into his.

Finally! He tasted her soft lips, her roving tongue. Thoughts yielded to sensation, urgent, inchoate. She was grinding against him. White heat between her legs spilled out onto his thigh. The world beyond her embrace receded to a meaningless mystery. The warmth between them increased. His prick pressed against her belly, almost unbearably hard. They stumbled, groping, bumping into the wall, the dresser, the mirror. They struggled in the grip of their desire, writhing, pawing each other like animals.

Backwards she walked, dragging him toward the bed, even as he pushed her ahead of him. She bumped against the edge and fell down on the mattress, looking up at him, eyes wide, legs tumbling open. Her breath, heavy with lust. He stared at her, paralyzed by a million desires. There were so many things he wanted to do to her. Kiss her, bite her, slather her cunt with his tongue until he was drinking her pleasure like a rivulet of wine... but the damn Belphegor Candle was burning.

There wasn't much time for foreplay. She knew it too. Mara pulled him down on the bed, kissed him, then pushed him back before he could get on top of her. With space between their bodies, she rolled up on all fours. *Of course*, Silfer thought; he was a devil, and she was Mara. There was no way they'd be doing this missionary style.

She looked back at him, cheeks flushed, eyes full of longing, burning like his own. Her wet cunt beckoned, a gorgeous gash beneath her ass. He took her hip in one hand, grabbed his prick with the other, guiding it in towards her aching sex.

Mara closed her eyes, ready to savor the exquisite shock of entry. She pictured Silfer's true form in her mind's eye – his wavy dark hair, his cute horns, his skin flushed red like the world's worst sunburn. She savored the essence of him, that mess of delicious impressions mingled with her love. She'd never wanted anyone so badly. And on the edge of penetration, she knew she'd never want anyone else ever again. When he fucked her, would the heat of their desire commingle, and burn up the world?

God, she hoped so. She felt him between her legs, on the edge of penetration. Her blood quickened, waiting, wanting.

Glass shattered. Warm liquid splattered over Mara's back. Something hit the floor with a *THUMP*! She turned to see Silfer, or rather, Todd, lying on the ground with half his head blown open, his brains decorating the floorboards.

"What!? No!" Mara cried. They'd been so fucking close!

Her door crashed open. Booted feet charged into her apartment, voices yelling "Go, go, go!" Two men in SWAT gear with automatic rifles swept into the room, scanning all angles. One stood above Silfer's dead vessel, training his gun on the annihilated skull; it seemed a superfluous precaution.

"Suspect is down," he said on the radio. "Repeat, suspect is down."

"Yeah, he's fucking done for," said the other officer.

Mara sat up on the bed, pulling a sheet over her nude body. Looking down at all those brains, she couldn't help but feel shocked; who'd have thought Todd would have so much going on inside his skull? Silfer's spectral body stood above the carcass, looking annoyed. He glanced at her and shrugged, smiling sadly, his eyes full of longing. Mara smiled sadly back at him. A dark-haired police woman knelt in front of her at eye-level, her face a mask of professional compassion.

"Are you okay, honey?" she asked.

Mara nodded.

"It looked like things were getting pretty rough in here," said the she-pig as she glanced at the clothes on the floor, the crooked mirror. "Did he... did he violate you?"

Mara sighed and shook her head. "No, he never got a chance," she said, trying to hide her disappointment.

"You know, you were really lucky," said another officer. "This maniac murdered his wife just half an hour ago. Smashed in her head with a hammer over at Home Depot. Luckily we glimpsed him through your window when we were checking out his house."

"Yeah," said Mara. "Lucky me."

"We should get you to a medic, make sure you're okay. Maybe you'd like to see a therapist?"

"No thanks," said Mara. "Maybe you could all just get the fuck out of my house?"

After the cops left, the pair stood over Todd's bloodstain.

"Looks kinda like Florida," Mara said, wondering how she was ever going to get Todd out of her floor. "I can't believe you killed Cara. I mean, I'm sure she had it coming, but still..." Mara tried not to smile. Murder wasn't supposed to be funny. "So what now? Any more ideas? Because I think our body count is getting kinda high."

Silfer sighed. "Well, I guess the whole possession idea is a dead-end. It's not just the problem with finding a suitable candidate, it's the expense. To possess someone, I have to burn a Belphegor Candle, and they don't come cheap. I'm just about out of cash." He sighed. Oh how he wanted to hold her, yet couldn't. "I suppose I can keep looking for a way to save you from Heaven. In the meantime, I can still visit you like this. I know it's hard, but it's better than nothing..."

"Yeah, I guess." Mara turned to him, frustration in her eyes. "Silfer?"

She looked around her apartment; he

was gone again. Christ, she needed to put a bell on that guy. She crawled onto her bed, hugging the demonic teddy bear from the carnival. It had been a long day.

The Belphegor Candle had burned down to a useless puddle of wax. Silfer fell back on the bed and groaned. His prick throbbed from ungratified desire. Even worse, his chest felt as if someone had wrenched it open, exposing his heart to a sucking, merciless wind. He *craved* her. It was worse than any of the tortures he'd ever inflicted, be it for pleasure or pay. To be so close to her, to touch her, feel her, to get within an inch of her delectable cunt, only to get pulled away again...it was agonizing. He honestly didn't know how they'd ever be together. If she ended up going to Heaven, then surely that was it. No devil could ever pass through the pearly gates – not unless something drastic happened to upset the status quo.

Still, at least he could spend time with her tomorrow. At least he could talk to her, see her smile. Even being with her in such a limited way was greater than any pleasure he'd ever experienced in Hell, including his sessions with the succubus sisters.

He pulled out his aching cock and started stroking it, thinking about her slender body, her luminous porcelain skin, her slick red lips. The look in her eyes as she'd knelt on the bed, so full of desire. Not just that, but everything about her. Her scintillating darkness, her delicious morbid dreams, the intoxicating essence of her. At the same time he thought about grasping her, crushing her close to him. Their mouths open, tongues intertwined, panting. His prick deep inside her, sheathed in her wetness, her hunger, her shuddering excitement.

"Mara," he gasped with ragged breath. His cum shot out and landed smoldering on the bed sheets. He lay back, catching his breath. His heart slowed to its usual rhythm. Even just jerking off to Mara was hotter than sex with other women. *At least I'll be able to see her tomorrow,* he thought. *At least this stupid fucking job is good for something.*

"You're fired."

"What?" said Silfer.

"You heard me," said Keith, Silfer's douchebag manager from Soul Trade LTD. "What did you expect? You've barely netted any souls all week. What're you even been doing up there? Going to rock concerts? Bird-watching? Romancing a mortal?" He laughed at his own joke, then turned serious again. "I'm sorry, Silfo," he added, with phony sincerity, "but we just don't have room around here for someone who's not pulling their weight. We can't afford to keep you on."

"What the fuck do you mean you can't afford me? According to that shitty fucking contract I signed, I'm an independent contractor. I have to pay all my own expenses!"

"Not all of them you don't," said Keith. "That cubicle you sit in isn't free. We still have to rent this building. And the last few days your takings have been so poor, you haven't even been able to cover the cost of us sending you to earth. I'm sorry Sil, I really am, but your days on the Soul Trade sales team are over. We need your desk space for someone more passionate. Someone with better time management skills and a positive attitude."

"Motherfucker!"

Silfer glared at Keith, his eyes flaring like embers exposed to the wind. His fingers clenched into fists and trembled. His scars itched, like they always did before a fight.

"Now just relax, okay buddy?" said Keith, stepping back. "It's nothing personal."

Silfer thought about shoving his thumbs into Keith's eyes and pulling his skull apart like a large Easter Egg.

"Not personal?" he growled. "Oh, it's just fucking business, right? Well, that's much better. I'm just not brainless enough to be another cog in the wheel, eh?"

Keith stood there silent, clearly afraid of what Silfer might do. Silfer glared at him a moment longer, then sighed.

"It's not fucking worth it," he muttered, turning to leave. He heard Keith exhale the heavy breath he'd been keeping inside.

Employees mumbled and moved out of the way, staring at Silfer as he left the cramped cattle pen of cubicles. Waiting by the elevators, he head Keith clap his hands and say "All right, show's over, back to work..."

At least Silfer would never have to hear that fucking voice again.

Outside he lit a cigarette and tried to ignore the endless static of the city. He didn't know if he wanted to cry or punch someone's face in. Probably both. More than anything, he wanted to see Mara. But without a Belphegor candle, without his shitty job, how the fuck would that be possible now?

10

Ecstasy in Decay

IT WAS THREE days since Mara had
heard from Silfer. Usually he was right there
at her door. The uncertainty tore at her.
The silence worried her. Maybe he'd given
up, felt their struggle wasn't worth it? Mara
didn't know anymore. She had enough trouble figuring out human men. Forget about
understanding the inner clockwork of a demon's mind. And yet, deep down, in spite of
her fears and doubts, Mara felt sure there
had to be something else keeping him away.

The sting of the shower felt good on her
muscles. Mara was thankful it was Sunday,
and she didn't have to worry about work.
She'd never be able to concentrate wondering what had happened, what *was* happen-

ing between the pair. She hated not knowing. But she was sure he loved her, and that would have to be enough for now. "Damn, where are you?" she said, her chest aching with desire and love for the absent demon.

Steam hung heavy in the air. Still Mara's skin felt chilled, her longing almost unbearable. She looked down at her birthmark, cursing silently to herself, hating God and his bullshit universe for doing this to her. What had she ever done to him to deserve such a curse?

"You must really fucking hate me," she said, wiping away the steam on the mirror.

Mara paused, her hand halfway across the glass.

"What the...?"

She watched letters appear in the fog, drawn by a formless finger, spelling a single strange word – *araM*.

"What?" she asked again, staring at the message. "What the fuck is 'Aram?'"

Then it clicked...*Oh, Mara.*

Instinctively she wrote back.

Silfer?

Mara! Yes, it's me. Something fucked up happened. I got sacked from my job! So

I can't come to earth in spectral form. At first I didn't know how I was going to contact you. But then I found this old book of spells. So I can talk to you through mirrors...

She watched as more steam accumulated and more words appeared.

Mara, I love you so much. I was scared you might think I'd abandoned you. And I can't even see you. I didn't even know if you were in the room or not! I've been writing your name for hours, just hoping you'd see it, having a shower or brushing your teeth or something

Mara couldn't believe it. She quickly wrote back.

I had no idea. No, I'm here. I knew something must have happened.

"Fuck," Mara said, watching the steam slowly vanish from the glass. She tried to write faster.

What are we going to do? How will you get back?

I don't know. I honestly don't fucking know. For now, this is the only way we can communicate. Mara, I miss you so bad.

I miss you too.

Don't worry, I'll keep looking for an answer. Until then, we can at least talk. It's better than nothing.

In his bathroom in Hell, Silfer placed his hand against the mirror, wishing he could reach into Mara's apartment and touch her. But he couldn't even see her, only his own forlorn reflection.

His hand print appeared before her, then faded as the last of the steam abandoned the room.

"Damn it!" Mara screamed. She stomped into the living room, pacing back and forth, furious not just at the situation but at bullshit politics in general. It was bad enough he was stuck in Hell, but she couldn't even hope to visit one day. When she died, they would only be further apart, and no mirror could ever connect them.

Mara lit a cigarette, trying to calm down. She just had to think. There had to be something. God and Satan couldn't be that smart. She'd read the Bible. It was all one big game. There was always a loophole, a clause on the page somewhere. She exhaled, looking around the room, thinking. Her eyes landed on her demented Hell bear.

He was lying on the floor beside her bed. He was always in places he wasn't supposed to be. She'd just plucked him from her underwear drawer that morning.

Feeling defeated, Mara snubbed her cigarette and wandered into the bedroom. "How did you get down there?" she asked, leaning over to pick him up. Crouching down, she saw the box, remembered the pages that had started this whole thing. The thing that had brought Silfer to her.

Mara sighed, sitting on the floor, pulling the box out. She ran her fingers over the smooth black surface, feeling the warmth from inside. It reminded her of Hell. Of Him. It was only late morning, but all Mara could do was crawl back into bed and sleep.

The shiver of longing vanished, licked away by a familiar flame creeping around her ankles, wrapping upwards around her torso. As the fire began devouring her, it traveled quicker, climbing her spine, filling her vision with embers. Coating her skin in powdery ash. Seven hungry tongues of red filled her mouth, spilled down her throat, and coiled inside.

Mara let it have her. She was too tired to fight. Let the fire consume her, she thought; it could only improve her situation. In the dream she saw the pages falling down around her, one after another, resting at her soot-blackened feet. Inside her their mystery faded, their knowledge burned sharp and bright. Suddenly Mara knew the pages as they knew her. She could see them for what they were – a prayer written by a thousand hands, but directed by a solitary dark one. They wanted her to read, to see. She beheld a crack in the sky, a hole in the earth. She saw the veil covering humanity's eyes burned away, revealing this world as nothing more than a badly drawn illusion.

The narrow tongues crept up from deep inside her belly. They twisted in her mouth, telling her the words. The ash, soft on her skin, comforted her. Embers in her head ignited fury at the creators of existence and the games they played. All she had to do was open her lips, say the words, and it would be done. The heat built up inside her, engulfing her from within, urging her to read, to speak as it could not. Mara exhaled, breathing out fire that scorched her lungs and blistered her skin.

Mara threw herself up in bed, gasping for air.

"Fucking water," she gagged.

Stumbling to the kitchen, Mara pressed her mouth under the faucet, sucking down water as if she hadn't drunk in days. She fell to the floor, resting her face on her knees, trying to slow her heart.

The pages...

Mara could be their mouthpiece if she desired. All she had to do was let them in. Mara decided then, that if she couldn't go to Hell, she would bring Hell to *her*.

With bare feet moving over cold wood, Mara stepped into her bedroom and crouched down. The box sat, waiting. A most patient consort. She fell to the floor and pulled the thing out, paused before opening it. She didn't know what to expect. She saw Pandora's box and all its curses rushing out into the world. This would be the hardest part of all.

Mara closed her eyes, thinking about the severity of her actions. Now she knew what the pages could really do, and she couldn't forget it. Speaking their words would birth the apocalypse – and mend her heart. The idea felt overwhelming. Such a dream colliding with reality was always harsher than one could anticipate. She looked up at the Hell bear sitting on the side of her bed. She sighed.

"Well, Veles, here it goes," she said.

The bear looked at her, a flicker in its bottomless eyes like a candle down a well, as if silently encouraging her.

Without another thought, Mara quickly turned the lock and lifted the heavy lid. The pages fluttered, then lay still. She looked down, waiting, but felt nothing. She'd thought maybe hellfire would burst forth, demons might fly out, the sky blacken and the ground begin to shake. But the sun continued to shine in her window; the birds kept singing. All she heard was the tick of the clock and the traffic outside.

Mara brought the box up to the bed and sat cross-legged, going through the loose pages. The great "D" engulfed in a crimson inferno. The gold "H" twisted with a red dragon. Mara set them all out and studied each one. It was easy to forget they were just lines and scratches, nothing more, unless spoken. Mara had prepared herself, she was ready. Now she saw it wasn't that simple. One did not simply bring about the End of Days on a whim. It required planning and ritual. A sacrifice. Defiling.

"Damn it, fucking men," Mara grumbled, reading what had to happen next. "How the hell am I supposed to find one of the Damned?"

Mara didn't have time to go around checking behind every ear, examining every thigh for a birthmark similar to her own, a 666 to match her 777. Then she remembered the book, the one Silfer had summoned on the day their romance had truly begun. Her name had been in there, listed amongst the Elect. Surely there had to be a *Book of the Damned* as well. That would make things a lot easier.

"Okay, we'll figure this out," Mara said, comforting herself. She glanced at Veles; he'd moved to the nightstand so he could read over her shoulder as she continued to study the apocalyptic ritual.

"Okay buddy," she said. "Let's see here... first, we need to find this Damned soul, whoever he is. Then we need to...." Mara read further down the page. "Do this ritual..... Hm.... dark moon.... pentagram... chant... candles..... knife..... blood.... fuck." Mara shook her head. It always came back to a woman having something shoved up her cunt. Story of her life. She knew she'd have to deal with it. She knew she *could* deal with it. She saw Silfer in her mind's eye, and thought about him in Todd's body touching her. Coming so close, only to be taken away. If she'd been prepared to fuck Todd, or that junkie, or whoever, just to be with Silfer, she could fuck some stranger too, knowing what it meant. The Earth would open, the clouds part, and the armies of Heaven and Hell would have no choice but to march out. Angels and demons on earth. *Her* demon on earth.

"Silfer," she whispered.

Despite her worry at ending the world, she failed to keep a slight smile from stirring the corners of her lips. Her future felt brighter already.

Mara walked into the bathroom and turned on the shower, filling the small room with steam. She wrote across the wide rectangular mirror.

Silfer, are you there?

Mara?

Oh, good. Mara wrote quickly. *I know what to do.* She jotted out her plan, what she needed him to do. *Find one of the Damned. I'll collect him. The ritual in the pages can open up the gates. Both pearl and iron. They'll have no choice. Then...* Mara sniffed. She hated fucking crying. It made her feel weak. She told herself the warm water creeping down her face was from the steam, nothing more.

Together, both wrote simultaneously over the top of each other.

Silfer promised he could find a name. Mara stood in front of the mirror, watching the damp white shadows fade until it was just her reflection staring back, eyes red, skin blotchy. She turned away, feeling relieved but guilty. She hadn't told him what the ritual entailed, just that she needed one of the Damned. He'd probably assumed it was for bloodletting.

"Damn it," Mara whispered, thinking about the idea of it all. Some asshole's worm between her legs. Whatever. She'd fuck this stranger, sit his throat, then never again.

She walked back into her bedroom. It had been a long day. The sun was falling. Shadows woke up and stretched across the floor. Mara sat in the window with Veles looking out at the calm city.

"Fuck this place," she told the bear, exhaling smoke through the screen. None of it seemed to matter, even though she knew it should. Humanity, the world, should matter more than anything. Yet Mara felt nothing for it, not pity or remorse. Everything paled in comparison when she thought of eternity among the burnt ruins with her lover.

"That'll be nice, huh, Veles?"

Mara petted the bear absentmindedly; his normal snarling expression curled into a jagged grin.

11

Sin for Satin

SILFER TOOK A deep breath. Mara's plan was apocalyptic – literally. Most sane devils would run a mile from it. It should at the very least have given him pause. But it didn't. He knew in his bones he wanted to be with her, no matter what, even if he had to burn down the cosmos to do it. Besides, didn't the cosmos sort of suck anyway?

He summoned the *Book of the Damned* that all devils had permanent access to. It appeared from the ether in a puff of smoke and landed in his hand. He flipped it open, searching for someone opposite Mara. Someone who'd been cursed since birth to enter the pits of Hell, no matter how they behaved themselves in life.

He quickly found a name – Sebastian Aubry. Apparently the guy lived in a Church somewhat close to Mara. *A church, huh?* That meant he was either a charity case or an actual priest. Just think about it – a damned priest. How hilarious. That jerk God really did move in some fucked-up mysterious ways.

Now that Silfer had Father Aubrey's details, he just needed to pass them on to Mara so she could perform the sacrifice. It pained him that he couldn't be with her to help, just in case something went wrong. What if the victim fought back? What if Mara got arrested? Shit, what if she got shot by the cops and ended up in Heaven?!

He needed to get her some helpers. Luckily there were always plenty of people on Earth keen to serve the powers of Hell. Silfer just needed to contact them.

He kicked himself for having lost his stupid job. It would've been perfect right now. He could always use the mirror magick, but that might take ages. What was he supposed to do, write messages on an occultist's bathroom mirror all day long until they finally noticed? What if they had poor hygiene and only showered every other week? He couldn't wait that long. He needed a faster way.

In the end he could only come up with a single option. It was risky in the extreme, and something he'd always avoided, but he had no other means of quickly visiting Earth.

Steeling himself, he took a bottle of blood from his refrigerator and splashed it on the floor. Using the fingers of a dead man's hand, he scrawled sigils in the gore across the lino. The fingers on the hand wriggled; he had to snap them to keep them still. He stood back, examining his work. It'd been ages since he'd dabbled with this shit. But the triangle was as good as it was going to get. It would have to be enough.

Silfer took another deep breath and stepped into the triangle. Allowing himself to be summoned to Earth was risky. He could end up anywhere, with anyone. A couple of stoned teenagers fooling around with *The Goetia*. A chaos magickian calling on the spirits of Aleister Crowley and Captain Crunch. The odds of getting someone who would serve his whims were perhaps quite low. Even worse, if they had genuine occult power, they could trap him for a while, like a migrant worker in a basement, sans passport. No one would know what had happened to him. No one would be around to hear him scream.

Maybe this is a bad idea, he thought.

He swallowed his worry and tried to focus on Mara's city. It was all energy, right? Power of mind? He knew where he wanted to go. Fuck the universe; he was going to be with her, no matter what.

Silfer closed his eyes, picturing Mara. Her apartment. The streets they had walked. The coffee shop she'd tried to ditch him at. As he focused a bright spark lit the air. His eyes snapped open. He looked down and saw the bloody triangle glowing neon red as he was sucked up from Hell towards the realm of Earth.

Silfer blinked his eyes. The room was thick with incense smoke. At his feet was a magickal triangle drawn in charcoal, surrounded by a bastardized mess of images from various grimoires both fake and genuine. Peering through the haze he saw three figures in a candlelit circle – a woman and two men, all dressed in cheap hooded robes from a Halloween store.

The bleached blonde woman was down on all fours, her robe thrown up over her haunches. A thin man knelt behind her, committing the blasphemous act of sodomy on her ass, while the third member of the trio – a fat man whose robe was almost bursting at the seams – stood off to the side, reading from an internet printout. In a slow, serious voice he butchered a series of demonic names.

"In nomine Astaroth and Satin... Beel-*ze*-bub and, uh, Apsu. Come here now, um... Tiamat? So I say!"

Silfer stood and waited. But the fucking and the chanting when on... and on. He didn't have all day.

"Hey," he finally said, when the three failed to notice him.

The chubby Satanist's head snapped up in response to the wicked whisper. He pushed his glasses further onto his wide nose, peering through the haze. His eyes went wide when he spotted Silfer in the gloom.

"Rick, Tracy, look!" he stuttered, pointing at the red-skinned devil.

"Shut up, Gary!" snapped Rick, the rite master. "I told you, for the ceremony to work, me and Tracy have to harness our sexual energies leading up to the moment of —"

"But the ritual... it *has* worked!" said Gary. "Over there!"

The fornicators followed the direction of the fat one's pig knuckle. They caught sight of Silfer and awkwardly froze mid-coitus, each wondering, perhaps, if they should cut out the sodomy or just keep going till the end. Rick opted for the former. Slipping his greased cock out of Tracy's ass and wiping himself off on the inside of his robe, he struggled to his feet and bowed before his sweet Satan.

Silfer sighed with relief. This was good. They weren't wizards out for power; they were worshipers, longing for submission.

"Great Lucifer!" Rick said, speaking in a pompous but weedy tone. "We are honored by your presence! Tell us your commands. We will serve you in all things. We offer you this maiden for your pleasure." He gestured to Tracy, still with her ass in the air. She looked at Silfer uneasily, as though being offered as a sacrificial fuck doll wasn't something she and Rick had talked about while he'd been lubing her up earlier.

"I don't have time for that stuff," said Silfer. "I'm here to give you a job."

"A job? So soon? Anything, oh Lord of Flies. Whatever your desire, we shall serve. Tell us, what is your will? Virgins? Burning churches? More sodomy?" Clearly Rick had been waiting for this his entire life. Now it was here. He couldn't wait to sin for Satan!

Silfer almost felt bad for them. This was too easy. "Good, great. Love the enthusiasm there. Rick, was it?"

Rick beamed – Satan had just said his name!

Silfer hurried on while he had their attention. "So the job. All three of your need to go help the...uh...the...The Chosen One of Darkness. She's going to be performing a ritual soon. Obey all her commands." He gave them Mara's name and address. The group continued to stare, unmoving. "Aren't you gonna write that down?"

Rick and Gary glanced at each other uneasily. Neither one of them had brought a pen into the ritual circle of protection. The stare-off lasted a few more seconds, then ended with Gary caving in; he was clearly the submissive one. Gingerly he stepped out of the circle and fished for a pen amongst a stack of Watain albums and melted candles on a nearby table.

"Don't worry," said Silfer, noticing his nervousness. "I'm not in the mood for slaughter today." Gary seemed relieved by this, but only slightly. Maybe Silfer's smile was too full of fangs to be comforting. He hurried back to the perceived safety of the circle.

"And... and will we be rewarded for this, oh Great Beast?" asked Rick, as Gary wrote Mara's details on the back of his internet printout of demonic names. "Will we become...living gods? Serving as your right hand with all the powers of Hell at our disposal? Bringing chaos and death to humanity? I want to see people crawl!"

"Yeah," said Silfer. "Of course. No problem. Just do whatever she tells you, without question. Then all my black gifts will be yours."

Gary and Rick slapped high fives, totally stoked; Tracy seemed skeptical as she wiped the excess lube from her ass.

Silfer stared at the trio. Normally he wouldn't trust a Satanist to light a black candle, but in this case he'd been left with little choice. They would just have to do.

Mara looked at the Satanists on her doorstep. So these were the guys Silfer had sent to assist her. Mara wasn't sure if she was grateful or irritated. By the looks of their rumpled polyester robes and faux silver pentagrams, they were obviously "Satanists" in the loosest sense of the word. She could only hope they didn't have stupid, made-up names like Damien Graves, Xander Black Thorn, or Drusilla Helvete. Still, she had to kidnap a priest and trigger the apocalypse; she needed all the help she could get.

"Uh, Hello?" she finally asked.

The trio traded glances, then shoved Gary up front. He cleared his throat and looked down at his shoes. "Are you the Chosen One of Darkness, ma'am?" his voice was so hushed Mara didn't think she'd heard him right.

"Am I the what?"

Tracy shoved her way between the two boys. Her rolling eyes said *Christ, do I have to do everything?*

"You're the Chosen One of Darkness, right?" she said. "The Devil told us we had to come serve you. So here we are, or whatever." Tracy's words were flat; her expression said she wasn't impressed by the "chosen one."

"Oh, right," said Mara. "Yeah, I'm the, uh, Chosen One of Darkness..." she dropped her voice and inwardly cringed as she repeated the silly title Silfer had given her. It might have impressed the Satanists, but it sounded like a screen handle for some teenage Emo on Tumblr. "Come inside," she said.

She ushered them in to her kitchen and told them the plan.

"Kidnapping?" said Tracy, looking uncomfortable. "I'm not sure..." she glanced over at the others, perhaps hoping that one would object. But they looked completely into it.

"Hell, yeah! We can kidnap a priest! Sure. Whatever you want, Dark One." They started slapping high fives and jumping around, knocking into Mara's uneven kitchen table. Mara was not amused.

"Great," she said. "You need to go to the Basilica of Saint Anne and get this guy. Bring him back here. We need to do this tonight. Think you can handle that?"

Rick and Gary were too busy celebrating their status as minions of darkness to pay attention, so Tracy took the address from Mara's hand.

"Anything else, Dark One?" said Tracy. She eyed Mara; Mara glared back. Neither woman seemed to enjoy the other.

"No, nothing else," said Mara.

Tracy turned to leave, grumbling something about having to do all the heavy lifting in the coven. The boys stumbled after her, bumping fists, keen to be the dogs of the apocalypse.

It was a beautiful summer afternoon.

The birds were singing sweetly outside the rectory. The late day sun draped the garden in heavenly yellow light. Father Aubry wandered through the green dead-heading white roses, whistling "Ave Maria." Looking around, he silently thanked God for the miracles of this world – the laughter of children across the street, the butterflies floating past.

There was nothing Father Aubry loved more than serving God. Not even the touch of a woman could penetrate the undying devotion he felt for his lord and savior Jesus Christ. He'd been born pure of body. He'd decided at fourteen – when all his classmates had been fucking anything with a hole between its legs – that he would stay that way forever. Father Aubry was thirty-three years old and a proud virgin. There was nothing he looked forward to more than teaching sexual education every second Sunday of the month in the church's basement. Letting teens know if they remained pure and chaste, God would open up to them in ways they couldn't possibly imagine.

He loved the looks of awe and wonder

on their faces when he described his own struggles. When he told them that no matter how far a woman spread her legs, she could never encompass him as deeply as Jesus could. In detail he told them all about the sexual wiles and attractions of women – their nubile bodies, their forbidden wet hollows, their sacrilegious art of fellatio – but always the message was the same: none of those things could ever compare to being showered in Christ's golden love.

Many of his students were fascinated with his in-depth discussions of carnal temptation. "Tell us more!" a young boy would say, as others sat entranced on the edges of their seats. Father Aubry was always more than happy to oblige. Of course the boys were always more curious than the girls about matters of religion, but Aubry didn't mind. There were plenty of places for women in the world, and the church wasn't one of them. Women belonged under their husbands, birthing babies. After all, they were born filthy, bleeding sinners. They might as well make the best of it.

Father Aubry came around the corner of the church. Three drab youths sat on the steps, smoking. "Can I help you?" he asked. The smoke from their cigarettes stung his eyes, but he tried to smile anyway. Maybe they were just looking for repentance?

A gawky young man snubbed out his cigarette, leaving a dark smear on the step. "Is your name Father Aubry?" he asked, drawing uncomfortably close.

"Yes. Are you here about –" that was all he got out. Father Aubry felt a single sharp knock to the head. He woke up twenty minutes later in the back of a car. His first sight was of a young woman's crotch. "Where am I... oh, what are you doing?"

The blonde temptress leaned down and laughed, blowing smoke in his face.

"Hush, you're fine," she said.

Father Aubry realized he was on the floor of a car bumping along. The young Jezebel was sitting in the back seat above him, laughing with someone in the front. They'd bound his hands and ankles with rope. The wayward whore in question wasn't wearing panties beneath her short black skirt. Father Aubry closed his eyes and prayed silently. He peaked through cracked eyelids; the cunt seemed to wink at him.

"You like what you see up there, father?" the sinful slut sneered.

Father Aubry went back to praying.

"Oh, turn that up, I love this song," she said, tapping a foot on his back in time with the horrible devil music filling the car.

"I have no money. Please, I'm only a priest," he begged.

"Sorry, can't hear you!"

The tramp laughed over the noise. It was hopeless. Only God could save him now.

A short time later the kidnappers were dragging Father Aubry bound and gagged up a flight of stairs.

"Oh Lord, please -" the filthy sock shoved in his mouth muffled his words.

"Shut the fuck up, father. Your God won't do shit. There's only one God and his name is Satin," Gary laughed.

"*Satan*," Rick corrected.

"That's what I said." Gary looked at him. "Satin."

"No dude, it's not -*in,* it's -*an*. 'Satin' is that shit they make women's panties out of. That shiny, cheap shit."

Gary looked mortified. "You mean...I've been saying it wrong *this whole time*?"

Tracy tapped her boot impatiently. "Come on. I can't move him by myself. Someone is going to notice, can we please?" She gestured down the hall toward their destination.

Gary tugged the holy man to his feet. Rick grabbed him from the other side to steady him up. Father Aubry stumbled along as they dragged him the rest of the way to Mara's apartment.

"What the fuck is this?" Rick asked, seeing a note taped to the front of Mara's door.

"Looks like an address."

"Yeah, no shit, Gravy."

"I really hate when you call me that. You know I like either Gary or Count Gzerski."

Rick ignored him. "We're supposed to take the priest here, I guess."

"Shit, really?" said Tracy. "We just brought him up three flights of fucking stairs. That bitch is so fucking bossy. I say fuck her. Let's just leave him here." Tracy pressed her foot gently down on Father Aubry's balls. He groaned into his gag.

"Nah, we can't just leave him, Tracy. You heard what Beelzebub said. We're supposed to serve The Chosen One of Darkness and then –"

"Fuck that little red fucker, Rick! You told me we were going to see Gwar tonight! What about that? It's like I don't even matter since you met that little cunt."

"But Tracy, the demon said –"

"Fuck you both!" shouted Tracy. "I knew I should have fucked that Mormon instead. His god would've never shown up!" She spat on the priest and stormed off, muttering to herself.

"Maybe you should go after her?" Gary asked. "It took ages to find a high priestess for the coven. Tracy was the only one game for all the sodomy..."

Rick cast an apathetic glance in Tracy's direction. "Don't worry about her, man. She's probably just on her period or something. I'll sweet talk her later. Come on, help me get this guy back in the car."

Father Aubry struggled and tried to call out, so Rick punched his teeth in, hauled him down the stairs, and threw him in the trunk.

In the dark of the hot, cramped space, Father Aubry whimpered. He felt warm blood dribble down his chin. Oh, where was

God when you really needed him? He knew this must be some sort of test. He just had to remain pure and strong. If he passed, maybe God would let him into Heaven after all. That was surely it. The 666 birthmark seemed to throb between his legs, the Mark of the Beast. Father Aubry tried to ignore it. He prayed harder than ever, focusing all his energy on the divine love of Jesus.

Silfer stepped into room 306 and sat across from Karla, his Infernal Employment Services Case Manager. She was still porky, still condescending, and still had those ridiculous sparkly nail extensions. Silfer couldn't stand the sight of her. And yet, he needed her. Now that Mara was bringing about the Apocalypse, he needed a new job. One that would put him on the front lines when all Hell broke loose.

"Hello, Mr. Incinerator," she said. "I guess your soul-collecting job didn't last very long."

"I guess not."

"You should have taken one of the other ones. They're all gone now."

"That's okay. I've got something else in mind. I want to join the Apocalyptic Army Reserve."

She looked at him as though he were fucking insane.

"Are you fucking insane, Mister Incinerator?" she asked. "Do you know the sort of people who work for the AAR? They're True Believers. Doomsday freaks. Total psychos! You seem like a relatively normal guy, even if you do have trouble holding down a job. Why would you want to get mixed up with people like that? Besides, the pay is terrible. You'd only make real money if the apocalypse actually happened. Then you'd get a shitload of danger pay. Not that you'd have time to spend it. The Archangel Michael would cut you down as soon as you rushed from the gates." She laughed. "Why am I even going on about this? The Apocalypse isn't going to happen anytime soon. Heaven doesn't want it, and neither does the Infernal Council."

"Maybe," said Silfer. "Still, I want this job. So can you get me an interview or not? I tried looking up the AAR's official website, but it was a dead end. There was nothing on there but videos of people being decapitated to the tune of death metal tracks. And when I called their recruitment hotline, it was nothing but terrified screaming and the sound of a buzzing chainsaw."

"And that didn't give you second thoughts about applying for a job?"

"No. So, are you gonna make the call, or what?"

Karla shrugged. "Fine. It's your funeral. And I'll still get my commission." She picked up the phone and cradled it under her chin while tapping on her keyboard, looking for the number. She dialed and continued to eye him while up waiting for someone to pick up. Her meaty hands trembled as the dial tone rang. She drew away from the receiver as a hoarse, bestial voice answered.

"Who is thisssss?"

"This is Karla Defenestrator from Infernal Employment Services. I've got a fresh recruit for you..."

She gave them Silfer's name, address, and all other pertinent details. For a time there was no sound over the line but crackling and occasional distant screams.

"Gooood," said the voice. "Fresh meat."

The call disconnected. Karla glanced at Silfer. "There," she said. "It's done. Have a pleasant life, Mister Incinerator. I doubt I'll be seeing you again."

Silfer didn't bother saying "Thank you." He left the building, lit up a smoke, and started walking. His heart hammered a little. The voice on the phone had been disturbing, to say the least. Everything he'd learned about the AAR made him want to avoid them like the plague. And yet, if he wanted to be first out the gates and into Mara's arms, he'd need to be on the front lines.

I wonder when they'll contact me? He thought. *Mara's ritual has to be almost ready to go. I need to be enlisted before she opens the gates. I should have told her to wait until I'm ready. It'll be a week at least before these AAR guys contact me. Assuming they're not too high off Angel Dust or Saints' Blood to pick up the phone. I wonder...*

His thoughts froze as a black armored van smashed through a pair of pedestrians and screeched to a halt in front of him.

The back doors flew open and three devils in balaclavas jumped out, waving crimson-plated AK-47s.

Silfer raised his hands instinctively. "I guess you guys must be from the AAR. You came faster than I expected."

The figures gave no answer. Swarming around him, two kept him in their sights while the third grabbed Silfer's hands and secured them behind his back with a plastic tie.

"Hey, what the fu—" Silfer didn't finish his sentence. The butt of an AK collided with his temple, knocking him down onto the pavement. Consciousness faded for a second, replaced with starry blackness. They placed a hood over his head. The rough fabric stank of blood and fear. He felt himself being lifted and tossed through the air. He landed in what was presumably the back of the van. Like the hood, it stank of terror and gore. The doors slammed with an ominous CLANG! As the engine growled and the van sped off, he thought only of Mara.

◆◄——————◆⊙◆——————►◄

"What the hell took so long?"

Mara was standing in the middle of an old grocery store that had been converted into a church and then abandoned a year later, after they'd arrested the pastor for tax evasion. A neon crucifix hummed behind her. In the middle of the former frozen food section was a large ritual circle, prepared as per the pages' instruction.

"We just got your note, O' Dark One," Rick said, bowing his head.

"Whatever, just put him in the circle." Mara flicked her cigarette butt as she focused on what to do next.

Gary dropped the weeping Father Aubry into the center of the pentagram. "This is really nice. Did you draw that out in dust first, or just spray paint it free hand? Good proportions."

Mara shrugged. "I don't know. Veles did it." She gestured to the Satanic teddy bear as she scanned one of the pages laid out on the floor.

Gary and Rick looked down at Veles sitting on a stack of crates. Its dead eyes burned into theirs and the boys had to turn away from its look of total malevolence.

"So what's with the venue change?" said Rick, keeping his eyes away from the bear at all costs. "You know you could have just called. It would have saved us ten minutes at least."

"Yeah, sorry," said Mara, not even bothering to try and sound sincere. "I skimmed over the pages first time I read them. Didn't notice the *defiling* had to be carried out in a desanctified church. Luckily this place was free. I would've called, but my phone was out of battery."

Rick grumbled, but Mara didn't give a shit; she had far more important things to worry about right now, like ending the universe.

She was short on candles, so she strung up some twinkle lights she'd found in the back room. "Okay, cut him loose. It says here I need to fuck him, then open his throat. And uh, whatever your name is –" Mara glanced at Rick – "You need to hand me the bowl so I can catch his blood. Then it looks like I draw on him with it... yadda, yadda, yadda... read this passage and... I guess that's it. Apocalypse, End of Days, whatever, we'll see." Mara rolled her eyes, shrugged off her dress and picked up the small kitchen knife. She just wanted to get this over with. Mara wasn't in the mood to fuck this man of God. She preferred devils these days.

Father Aubry remained gagged and bound, pleading, in the middle of the circle.

"Are you going to untie him or what?" Mara asked. "Hey, weren't there three of you earlier?" she said, just now noticing that Tracy was missing.

"Yeah, she had shit to do. Don't worry about it," Rick assured her, removing the ropes from the priest.

"Oh, please, please!" Father Aubry begged as the gag was removed.

"Don't be such a bitch, father," Rick said. Gary chuckled.

"Just hold him down." Mara was irritated enough she had to fuck this priest, but having to do it while he cried was even more pathetic. "Could you stop making that noise, please?" she asked.

"I don't know what you want, but I am a man of God and –"

"Not according to that mark on your thigh. Sorry, Father, but I need you more than God does at the moment."

She unwrapped the priest from his stark black cassock. Father Aubry wept harder as Mara straddled him. His limp little worm hardened to her warmth. She pushed him inside, slowly fucking him, feeling him move in and out of her damp cunt.

The harder he became, the deeper she drove him in. Mara had always had a thing for priests. Something about all the black, the forbidden nature of it all. But this priest, crying, pathetic, his hands clutching at her... she'd always thought it would be hotter than this. What a letdown.

"Jesus... no, Jesus. I am pure. I am pure. No!" Father Aubry struggled against the weight of Mara. Mara struggled to hold him inside her.

"Just fucking hold still," she said, grinding down on him harder, just wanting it over with. Gary and Rick looked on, watching the angry little woman fuck the Catholic priest on the floor of the old grocery store-turned-church. The neon blazed behind them, casting the scene in the calm blue light of the Holy spirit.

"Lord in Heav-*an*!" the priest gasped,

feeling the heat of Mara as she encased
him with her cunt, forcing him deeper each
time. The love he felt for Jesus rapidly began to pale in comparison to the raw sweet-
ness he felt blooming inside him. From the
center of his pelvis, through his holy vessel
and into the jezebel's cunt, it sang the song
of God. Father Aubry grasped for prayer,
but only sharp breaths escaped his gaping
lips.

Feeling it was time, Mara picked up
the knife. At least she got to stab him, because this whole defiling business was boring. Father Aubry opened his eyes and saw
the knife glinting with the reflection of the
glowing Jesus. He came, and Mara cut. She
pressed hard, making sure to nick all the
tubes beneath his thin skin.

A thick wet death rattle replaced the
priest's ecstasy. "Catch the blood, as much
as you can," Mara said, still sitting astride
the dying man. "Hey! The fucking bowl!"

Rick struggled to tear his eyes from
the naked woman and the mangled priest,
whose blood spilled out and curled around
his head, forming a sticky red halo.

"Hold up that page right there," said

Mara. She felt the dead priest's little horn fall out of her cunt as she bent forward to read the page:

Ol boaluahe g uml
ol boaluahe g kures
g cnila od gah
cacrg a uls c basgm
cacrg a undl basgm
ca el gohed

"Oh fuck."

Cherubiel had been performing his routine angelic rounds when he heard the devilspeak arise from the decadent church. As surprised as he was to hear the language of Hell being spoken by a human tongue, he was even more surprised when he recognized the words as coming from the *Codex Infernalis Futuatoris*, the most terrible and dangerous book in all the cosmos, which contained nothing less than a ritual formula for invoking the apocalypse. There were a number of such formulae floating around, but most were outrageously complex, requiring months of intense preparation, special artifacts, correct stellar arrangements, and so on, making them virtually impossible to complete. The ritual in the *Codex* was remarkable in its relative speed and simplicity; it was the apocalyptic ritual equivalent of pressing CTRL + ALT + DEL on a computer – it cut right to the chase.

"Fuck," said Cherubiel again. "I have to stop it!"

He still had a chance, so long as he acted quickly. He just had to interrupt the ritual before they could complete the invocation. He couldn't intervene himself, due to the Hezekiah Pact; his only option was to find a mortal champion to intercede for him.

He flew around the block, desperately seeking any mortal he could find. In a ray of light he appeared before the first one he saw, a young woman in a black beret and a striped cardigan.

"Mortal!" he said. "You have been chosen to prevent the apocalypse! I command you –"

"Excuse me?" said the woman. "You can't *command* me to do anything. As Sartre says, all human beings are born free, *thrust* into life and condemned to freedom! Even a crazy person receiving commands from an angel gets to choose to obey them or not. The only way you'll get me to do what you want is by engaging me in reasoned debate."

Taken aback, the angel peered at the woman, noticing a university textbook tucked beneath her arm, entitled *Beginner's Philosophy: From Plato to Nietzsche*. With a curse on his lips against those blasted Existentialists, the angel flew off in search of another champion, while the vile devil-speak continued to flow from the desanctified church.

On the other side of the block he found someone who looked promising, a bear of a man with long black hair and a beard. He looked like a modern warrior. He even had a patch on his denim jacket that said "angel" on it. Surely he'd help!

In a flash of light Cherubiel appeared before him.

"Mortal!" he said. "The apocalypse is at hand. You must –"

"The apocalypse, huh?" said the man, his eyes wild with amphetamine madness. "That's fucking cool. You want me to help get it started, you *faggot*?"

The angel, again, was taken aback. Taking a closer look at the man, he saw he was wearing a Dark Funeral T-Shirt with the slogan "Teach Children to Worship Satan." The patch on his jacket didn't say "angel" – it said "*Morbid* Angel."

"Oh great, a fucking metalhead," said Cherubiel with a sigh.

Not wanting to waste any more precious time – for the ritual invocation was almost complete – Cherubiel flew off again, stopping at an alleyway in which a trio of hobos were cavorting drunkenly around a burning oil drum, singing a funeral hymn for some guy called "One-eyed Bill," who'd apparently died of a heart attack a few days previous.

He appeared to them in a blaze of light.

"Mortals!" he said. "Though ye be humble, you have been chosen to help avert the apocalypse. Go ye into that church, and stop the wicked rite from being completed!"

The hobos looked at him with glazed eyes.

"You got any cigarettes, man?" one of them said.

"Hey, aren't you Michael Bolton?" said

another.

"You got any booze? Any spare change?"

On the verge of despair, but with no time to lose, Cherubiel quickly promised them five cartons of cigarettes and three bottles of Captain Morgan if they hurried up and stopped the apocalypse. He also told them *yes,* he *was* Michael Bolton, just to shut them up.

"Here," he said. "Take these. They'll help you against the powers of darkness."

He handed them some monkish robes and blessed swords anointed with the blood of the saints. They equipped themselves in the guise of holy soldiers and rushed towards the decrepit supermarket-cum-church-cum-apocalyptic ritual site, ready to kill in the name of rum, tobacco, and Bolton.

Mara kept reading from the book; the invocation was almost done.

Ol boaluahe g uml
ol boaluahe g kures...

The door to the church flew open, almost breaking her concentration. Dry leaves blew in; it was only the wind.

She kept mumbling her way through the rite. Despite the flaccid cock pressing on her inner thigh, the sting of blood in her nose, she'd never felt more sure of anything. Gut instinct moved her forward. She looked but didn't see; only the outcome mattered. Mara drew assorted symbols on the priest's forehead, while the two Satanists stood by, staring in fascination and lust.

Coming to the end of the last page, Mara exhaled. "There, I think that's –"

She was interrupted by the sound of feet moving over linoleum. She looked up to see three men rushing into the room through the open door, dressed in monkish robes and brandishing gleaming swords. For a moment they looked like holy warriors – until she saw their filthy faces, rotting teeth, and drunken eyes.

"For Michael Bolton!"

"For Captain Morgan!"

"For One-Eyed Bill!" they cried in ravaged voices.

"God damn it," said Mara.

She rushed to throw on her dress, while Gary's head thudded to the ground, severed by the strike of a holy hobo's sword. Arcs of blood exploded from the neck stump and splattered the wall's neon crucifix, whose light took on a dark and gory sheen.

"Gravy!" cried Rick, backing away in terror. Piss ran down his leg as the holy hobos surrounded him. "Tracy was right," he cried. "We should've just gone to see Gwar!"

A blade flashed and his head rolled off into the shadows where Gary's had gone. The floor obviously had a slant to the left.

The holy killers closed in on Mara. She backed into the center of the ritual circle, stepping over Father Aubry's drained corpse. The blood was warm on her bare feet. She clutched Veles to her chest, the gore on her arms seeping into his foul fur.

Mara's heart hammered and a voice of fear spoke in her mind. Could this be the end? Would she be murdered in the name of a cheesy rum mascot before the apocalypse could even start? And what about the ritual? Had it even worked?

The Earth began to tremble as if in answer. The holy hobos paused, looking at each other. Mara threw Veles at one of them and ran. Behind her, she heard screams and ripping. "Dear god, no! The bear!" one cried. "Get it off, get it off! My eye! AH!"

Shooting a glance over her shoulder, Mara saw the shadow of the bear on the wall, towering, monstrous, splattered with fresh gouts of gore.

She rushed out into the street, jumped into the Satanists' car, and drove toward home. She wasn't worried about Veles. He'd probably be on her bed when she got back. He was cool and industrious like that.

A black disc slid over the sun as Mara pulled up in front of her building. On the sidewalk frogs groaned. The clicking of insect wings rose up and drew closer. After scrubbing her insides out in the shower, Mara sat in her window smoking a cigarette, watching the sky blacken and the river turn red. It wouldn't be long now.

12

Blessed Black Wings

SILFER BLINKED HIS eyes as the hood was torn away. He was on his knees in a particularly ugly part of Hell. A wasteland of ashes and bones stretched as far as the eye could see. Rolling dunes of death covered parts of the horizon. The sky was a whirl of spiraling clouds the colors of ruby and sulphur. There was no sign of vegetation, no sign of anything, but for a skeletal yew tree.

In front of the tree were three soldiers, presumably the ones who'd kidnapped him. They wore camo gear the color of flesh and blood. The uniforms were designed to help them blend into the mountains of dead mortal bodies that would festoon the earth when Judgement Day came. They all had tattoos of impaled angels on a fiery background, no doubt some sort of regimental emblem, accompanied by their motto - "angel rectums do bleed." Instead of ears, all three had nothing but nubs of scar tissue. They smoked cigarettes rolled from thin slices of human epithelium; the smoke stank of death.

"So you wanna join the Reserves, do you, mate?" said one of them. He was the shortest, but easily the scariest, with silver-plated teeth and scars galore. Looking into his eyes made Silfer's hackles stand on end. His heart hammering, he fought to conceal his fear. He'd grown up in the Ninth Layer, he could handle himself. Plus, he had to do this, for Mara. He could do anything for her, endure anything. Her love made him invincible, he was sure of it – so long as they didn't shoot him in the head.

"Yeah, I want to join," he said. "I want to be there when the gates open, first in line."

The soldiers grinned, impressed with his fervor. "You've got a good attitude," said the scary short one. "Let's see if you've got what it takes."

Silfer decided to play it safe and not ask

questions. The soldiers chain-smoked, leering at him as though he were a fresh ham in a butcher shop. Trying to scare him, probably. Occasionally they would whisper in low sinister voices and burst out laughing. He only heard stray words and phrases here and there.

"Lips... severed... blood all over...no teeth left... like a stuffed turkey... eyeballs... cut them, cut them..."

The laughter rose around the words like flies around death.

A billowing cloud of ashes and bone dust appeared in the distance, heralding the approach of another black armored van, careening wildly over the dunes. It came to a growling halt. Three masked figures with crimson-plated AKs stepped out. They went to the back of the van and opened the doors. Silfer gulped when he saw what lay inside. "Time for your first test, rookie," said the short one. "The Trial of Blood."

They were only human souls, but they were still scary. All three looked like they'd been skinheads in life. They wore acid wash jeans, wife-beaters, boots and braces. Their arms were covered in Nazi propaganda –

swastikas, eagles, the usual shit. Of course, none of that worried Silfer. He'd worked for almost six months torturing Nazis down in the eighth layer.

No, what was scary about these souls was what had happened to them *after* they'd gotten to Hell. Infernal science had altered them. They were now well over seven feet tall. Their muscles would put 1980s Arnie to shame. The scientists had adorned their bodies with vicious modifications: spiky metal knuckles, bayonet nipples, barbed wire wristbands. Their eyes were bestial, deranged. One lacked a human head; it had been replaced by that of a bulldog, jaws frothing with murderous hunger.

"Meet your new playmates," said the short soldier. "Your task is simple: survive."

The skinheads moved in and fanned out, silent but for their rasping breath.

Silfer scrambled to his feet, his arms still bound. "You gonna untie me?" he asked, striving to keep a hint of panic from rising in his voice.

"Sorry, mate," said the soldier. "You'll have to sort that out yourself."

"Fucking cunts," hissed Silfer.

The soldiers just laughed and cracked open beers, watching.

Silfer felt adrenaline surge through his blackened veins. His old scars ached, burning with eldritch energies, the gift of a childhood he preferred to forget. His chest swelled, his body grew. Thick black hairs sprouted below his waist and all over his forearms; fingernails and toenails morphed into claws; his mouth became almost a muzzle, bestial, drooling. The bonds on his wrists snapped, setting him free just as the first of the skinheads rushed him.

Silfer ripped the guy's throat out with a swipe of his talons. Soon the others were on him. The bulldog-headed skinhead bit into his forearm, savaging the flesh to the bone. The third one slipped in behind him, placing one arm around his neck and another behind, trying to choke him out in a sleeper hold. Silfer grabbed the guy's balls with his tail and gave them a twist. The skinhead screamed and stumbled backwards, letting go of his neck. At the same time Silfer jammed his fingers in the bulldog's eyes, plucking them out. Vile jelly squirmed around his knuckles.

The mutant stumbled back, howling in pain, hands flying up to cradle blinded eyes. Silfer kicked him hard between the legs, missing the balls, but slicing up into his inguinal canal with razor-sharp toes. For a moment he wore the guy's chode like a slipper. He withdrew his foot in a shower of gore.

Silfer howled in pain as the third skinhead's razorblade-encrusted fist connected with his ribs from behind. Agonizing, almost paralyzing pain spread out from the site of the impact. Silfer spun around, swiping but missing. The skinhead swung too, catching Silfer in the face, ripping his cheek. Another blow came but Silfer saw it coming. He caught his foe by the wrist and rammed his palm into his elbow, cracking the limb like a tree branch. Blood and bone erupted from the splitting epidermis.

The skinhead screamed. Silfer twisted the limb, wrenching it free. He took the bony end and jammed it deep into the skinhead's face, once, twice, and again, driving him down to the ground and continuing to stab until the Nazi's severed forearm was embedded in one of his eye sockets.

Silfer stood up, panting. The three soldiers laughed and clapped.

"Nice work, mate," said one. "But don't get too relaxed. You're not done yet."

Silfer turned to see the two other skinheads getting up. One without eyes, the other without a throat. As souls in Hell, they could never quite die. They rushed him again, thirsty for slaughter.

Cherubiel watched as the demonic teddy bear devoured the last of the hobos. The feasting had gone on for quite some time, but the angel had been unable to look away. It wasn't that he was shocked by the violence – he'd seen much worse. He'd even done much worse, for angels were not just God's messengers, but his murderers too. Who else had slaughtered all the firstborn in Egypt and murdered all the Sodomites in Sodom? No, it was not the violence that held him in place, paralyzed and twitching as the earth began to quake. It was the bear's eyes, gleaming with ancient malevolence.

Cherubiel gulped as he saw the true nature of the Bear – or thought he did.

"You," he said. "You!"

The bear opened his mouth – but not to speak. Instead he inhaled, sucking the angel's intangible form down his gullet and into his fathomless innards. Cherubiel screamed, his essence stretching out like taffy before stubbornly disappearing beyond the bear's bloody maw.

The bear laughed, then burped, then slouched toward Mara's apartment.

Silfer slumped to his knees, coughing up blood. Shredded, the skinheads could only wriggle like disfigured worms. A soldier began burying them under the ashen plain, like a cat burying shit. There they would remain until doomsday – which wouldn't be that long, assuming Mara's ritual was on track.

Silfer sighed; he was still alive, barely. Covered in bruises, lacerations, and bite marks, Silfer shrank down into his normal devil shape, exhausted. His scars ached and bled now that the eldritch energy had left him.

"Nice trick," said one soldier, taller and uglier than the others. "Haven't seen that before. Where'd you learn it?"

"From a self-help tape," said Silfer. "*Unleashing the Violence in You.*"

The soldiers laughed.

"A comedian," snuffed the short one. "That's good. We love a laugh. Let's see if you can laugh after the next test."

"The next test?" said Silfer, far from overjoyed by this latest revelation.

"That's right. The Trial of Sacrifice."

Silfer didn't like the sound of that. He liked it even less when four figures were dragged from the back of the second van. The first three were naked and female, bags covering their faces. Silfer recognized them at once; he'd know those naked bodies anywhere. He'd spent hours on top of them, underneath them, inside them. They were none other than the succubus sisters, their bodies ripped and chewed raw at the crotch.

Silfer's pulse pounded. Instinct told him to grab a soldier and rip out his throat, but he knew he'd get gunned down before he even took two steps. Plus, he had to join these bastards even if he hated them. He gritted his teeth, swallowing his anger and disgust. The soldiers tore the hoods from the heads of the succubi.

"I believe you know these lovely ladies," said the short one.

"Sil?" said DeeDee. "Sil, what's going on!?"

"Help us!" said Kiki.

Spitting bullets into the air, the barking of a rifle silenced their pleas. "Shut up."

The sisters fell silent, eyes wet with fear. The short soldier stepped up to Silfer and handed him a bowie knife. "Here you go, mate," he said. "Time to open these girls up. Demonstrate your commitment to AAR."

Silfer took the knife, looking at the quivering devils in the dirt. Could he kill the sisters? He didn't love them, of course, but they were his friends. They didn't deserve to die like this. And yet, killing them was his only chance of being with Mara. Was his love so relentless and cruel? Could it make him do something so utterly awful?

"We're waiting," said the short one.

Silfer glanced over at him, irritated. He could only hope it would be that short fucker at the end of his blade one day.

He turned back to the sisters. If he was going to do this, he couldn't doubt himself. He'd give them a clean death, no hesitation. Stepping forward, he opened DeeDee's throat, then Kiki's, then CeeCee's, in three quick swipes. The blade, so sharp, didn't falter. The sisters fell into a scarlet pile before him. Silfer felt tears burning at the edges of his eyes, but it was done. He was one step closer to being with Mara. He knew he would offer endless blood, endless bodies, for their love. Nothing else mattered.

There was no laughter from the soldiers this time, only looks of grudging respect.

"One more to go," said the short one. They ripped the hood off the fourth figure, though Silfer had already guessed who it was – Rust, his so-called best friend. The guy was a bit of a tool, but Silfer still cared about him; this wouldn't be any easier.

"Silfer?" he said. "What... what's going on?" He saw the knife. "Please, no... I'm too young to die! I like this incarnation! I still haven't convinced Donna to suck me off in the stationary cupboard! Silfer, buddy, please –"

His voice became a gargle of blood. Silfer tossed the bowie knife into the dirt. His heart felt wounded, almost punctured. But deep inside it was somehow serene, filled with an image of Mara. How could he be so calm while becoming a monster?

"You still need that knife," said the short one. "There's one more sacrifice to be made."

Silfer's heart quickened as a terrible thought crossed his mind. Had they somehow found out about Mara?! No, that wasn't possible. Besides, they could never get her into Hell, even if they wanted. Could they?

"The next sacrifice is the ultimate test," said the short one. "The Trial of Flesh. Offer a part of yourself."

Silfer breathed a sigh of relief. Self-mutilation. That was easy. He could do that.

"You need to cut your cock off."

Silfer's eyes went wide. Were these guys fucking serious? He couldn't fuck Mara without a cock! But if he didn't do it, these guys may very well kill him. Would Mara love a eunuch? This was turning into a total disaster.

The soldiers started laughing.

"Just joking, mate," said the short one.

"We don't really expect you to do that. That would just be sacrilegious. Just cut off your ears."

Silfer breathed a second sigh of relief. Of course it had been a joke. He should have seen right through it. In hindsight, it was obvious; all these guys were missing their ears.

He picked up the filthy blade, red with the blood of his former friends, and started cutting. The pain was excruciating. Fresh blood rolled down his neck. He did not cry out, nor flinch from the pain. Finally, two slices of ear lay twisted and red in the palm of his hand.

"Alright!" said the short one. "You're in. Private Silfer Incinerator."

The soldier's words had a terrible resonance. The whirling sky became even more chaotic and fearsome. Sickly clouds spun in dizzying gyros. The ground opened up nearby, yielding to a fathomless void. A figure flew out on blessed black wings.

Apollyon, thought Silfer, *the Angel of the Bottomless Pit*.

The fallen angel landed in front of him, regal, imperious. Like his heavenly kin, he resembled a stud from the cover of a romance novel, save that his eyes were brimming with infinite malice. He wore boots and gloves made from the skins of other angels he'd slain during Lucifer's uprising. Otherwise he was dressed much like Colonel Gaddafi, in a gaudy purple military uniform. Pearl-handled revolvers hung from his belt. Hideous locusts with human faces hovered behind him, some like painted tramps, others wearing corpse paint. He held out his flawless hand expectantly.

"Huh?" said Silfer, momentarily stunned. "Oh, right." He pressed his severed ears into the angel's palm. *I guess I'm sort of like Van Gogh,* he thought, giddy from blood loss. *Giving up my ears for the sake of love...*

The angel, in silence, squeezed the ears, then opened his hand, revealing a pair of shiny dog tags on a chain. Silfer took them and placed them round his neck

"Congratulations, mate," said the short soldier.

Lightning crashed. The angel uplifted his face to the distance. Joyous laughter escaped his mouth as the sound of a trumpet tore through space and time.

Silfer's entire body trembled. "Mara," he whispered. "She did it…"

"You picked one hell of a bloody good time to join up," said one of the soldiers. "Looks like the Apocalypse is now!"

13

Bloodlands

WHEN THE LOCUSTS started climbing on her screen and the wind blew the smell of charred carcasses into her apartment, Mara shut the window. She knew it was only a matter of time before the armies of Heaven and Hell would invade and tear the world apart. Mara couldn't wait! It was going to be so exciting. She thought about her dream. About Todd and Cara next door. Well, they were already dead, so that part wasn't coming true. Still, she wanted to go out and watch the downfall of man.

Mara tucked Veles into a bag so he could see too. She didn't bother locking up as she left. In the hallway, she heard her neighbors praying behind closed doors. One man ran up the stairs and grabbed her by the shoulders.

"Don't go out there. Oh, God!" he was sweaty with a red smear across his cheek, his eyes wide with panic and fear. Mara's calm appearance must have startled him, because he released her and backed away before running back in the other direction.

Mara clicked her tongue. "What a bitch."

He hadn't seen anything yet. The apocalypse had only just started. What could scare a middle-class white man so badly? He'd probably heard the economy was crashing. Mara doubted anyone was even dead yet; it had only been thirty minutes.

Outside, Mara saw cars speeding past. Groups of religious fanatics marched through the streets. Fire seeped from a long gash in the sky. It didn't seem so bad. Besides the crunching of insects under her boots, the city didn't seem that different. Mara kicked an obese toad off the sidewalk and headed past Todd and Cara's. It was eerily quiet. Since they'd died, kids had spray-painted their house. The colors looked nice in contrast to all the white. Mara decided the graffiti was an improvement.

"The end is nigh!" A street preacher in a black trash bag screamed.

Mara stopped to listen. He was jumping up and down, his voice hoarse. She couldn't decide if he was really scared or really excited that he was going to die.

"Have you repented?" he asked her.

"I've got to go," Mara said. She hated when people talked *to* her about religion. She preferred for them to talk *at* her. It made it easier to walk away.

"Young lady, young lady, stop! The End of Days is upon us. Please!"

He grabbed onto her arm as she tried to pass. Mara stopped, annoyed but sympathetic. He was crazy, but maybe he was only worried about her immortal soul.

"What?" she asked.

"Donate to the cause?" he said, eyeing her greedily.

"Un-fucking-believable. The world is ending and you want money?!" Mara wrestled her arm away from the trash bag preacher. He called for her to come back, but his shouts were lost among the cries of the city as death rolled in.

Streaks of fire fell around her, lighting her way through the chaos. It wasn't as fun as her dream had been. People were much dumber in life. Not only were people stealing televisions, they were trying to sell them to other looters who'd gotten there late. Women stood nearby, filming the whole thing on their cell phones, threatening to call the police.

No fat women were eating yogis over at the yoga studio. Mara stopped by the coffee shop, but it was empty. Another let down. She didn't even see any crazy people, just angry, stupid people. Across the street, the museum looked intact, more or less. Not one horseman in sight.

"Maybe we should just go home," she said, looking down at Veles, who seemed even more unimpressed than she was. "You've probably seen all this before. I don't know. I just thought it would be different, you know?"

As she walked home, Mara wondered about Silfer. How long would it take for him to find her amidst the chaos?

That's what's missing, she realized. She'd only done this whole stupid end of the world thing and fucked that cunty priest to bring Silfer here. But where was he? Maybe he hadn't been able to get in with the army. Maybe he'd just changed his mind?

As she walked toward the entrance to her apartment, she longed for him so completely she didn't even notice the flames whipping up from the earth.

"Get to the front, Private. You're angel fodder."

Silfer tried to hide his glee as they pushed him to the front ranks. Hell's creaking gates were about to burst wide open. The metal was seething, the adamantine chains fit to snap as the barriers between the dimensions began to give way. Gabriel's trumpet tore through space and time like a razor through skin. The time was at hand. Soon he'd be in Mara's arms!

He wasn't the only excited one. Hell's army loomed behind him, vast and terrible. The soldiers of the AAR were in the vanguard, led by Apollyon himself, surrounded by his retinue of hideous locusts. Behind the vanguard loomed countless other dev-

ils, hell beasts and unyielding abominations
of war. Only the Morning Star himself, a no-
torious prima donna, was absent from proceedings.

What a wanker, thought Silfer.

He was dressed like the rest of the AAR
in a set of combat fatigues the color of flesh
and blood. A black ballistics mask covered
his face, his eyes glowing red through the
sights. He carried the modern equivalent of
the ancient devil's pitchfork, the Pitchfork
L333, a crimson rifle with a uniquely Hellish design.

His heart hammered hard. Terror was
there, but serenity too. Somehow his longing for Mara insulated his inner self from
fear. He knew he could overcome anything
to get to her. Short of death, of course. And
even then, who knew?

The gates ripped open, revealing an
open wound in reality. The cosmos was
torn, bleeding. A stench both bitter and
sweet, with a hint of ozone, blew through
the rift. Silfer charged through the gates
with the rest of Hell's army. The sound of
the troops was almost as loud as that of reality tearing apart.

"Fuck! Those flying cunts are here already!"

A devil next to Silfer went down in an explosion of blood, obliterated by angelic fire as Hell's army rushed from the Hellmouth. In the tattered sky above, radiant holes led to battle-ready Heaven. Angels and their lackeys swooped down, unloading magazines filled with blessed bullets. Silfer fired into the sky almost at random, unleashing incendiary rounds. An angel exploded, wings on fire as it fell. The muzzle flare from Silfer's rifle looked like a pitchfork written in fiery blood.

Apollyon took flight and engaged with the angels. The air was a fuckfest of slaughter. The sound of dimensional catastrophe competed with a hundred thousand screams. Silfer didn't want to be here. He rushed toward Mara's apartment, hoping to escape from the melee before more angels descended to the Earth.

Someone grabbed his shoulder. "Oy, cunt!" roared the short officer. "Where do you think you're going?"

Silfer shot him in the kneecap and shoved him off. Rushing through the fray, he came out onto the street. With a backward glance he saw the soldier impaled by an archangel's spear.

"That's for DeeDee and the others, shithead," said Silfer.

He sprinted as fast as he could, trying to get as much distance from himself and the battle as possible. Wherever he went there was yelling, crying, the sound of crumbling matter. Buildings succumbed to yawning sinkholes in the ground. The sky was like a tattered banner, oozing disgustingly radiant light from the perforated Heaven. From the interdimensional holes came the sound of angels singing with the souls of the blessed, praising the sacred name of God – "*Steve.*"

"Huh," said Silfer. "Always thought it would be more impressive than that."

Thankfully, the singing was mostly drowned out by the calamitous warfare down on Earth and the sound of Gabriel's trumpet.

"Geesh that angel can really blow," said Silfer to himself.

He noticed a misty blood rain starting to fall. He rushed on, hoping to find Mara before all Heaven broke loose.

Silfer turned a corner and stopped in his tracks. The ground in front of him erupted. A massive Hellworm rose up before him, its mouth a puckered cunt. Wet crimson arms branched out from the labia, grasping for things to devour. He gave the monster a wide berth, allowing it to inhale some hapless humans who looked like they'd just come out of a rock concert. Their Gwar t-shirts vanished into the Hellworm's vertical maw.

As much as he wanted to stay and watch the Hellworm have dessert, he was just a few blocks from Mara's apartment.

He raced past the building site where he and Mara had first met, then leapt back as bullets grazed the ground in front of him. He turned to run, but more bullets slammed into the ground behind him, penning him in. Two angels descended from the upper level of the building site, swooping in on dove-like wings. Their golden uniforms looked like the creation of some fascist John Paul Gaultier from an alternate dimension.

"Time to die, you red devil bastard!" said one of them.

Silfer glared at them through the slits of

his ballistics mask. He could maybe shoot one, but the other would kill him. A surge of rage swelled inside him as he realized he was screwed. This was it. He'd never see Mara. Some douchebag angels were going to make him dance, then make him die. He took off his suffocating mask and sighed.

"I love you, Mara," he said. "I'm sorry."

"Mara?" laughed an angel. "She your hell whore? How sweet."

Silfer glared at him. "You gonna shoot me or talk me to death, fuckface?"

The angel glared and raised his rifle. Shots exploded. So did the angel's head. His comrade collapsed a split second later, shot through the heart. Silfer's eyes went wide with confusion. He watched as another angel emerged, a familiar one.

"Ofaniel?" he said in disbelief.

"The very same," said the angel.

"Wow," said Silfer. "I mean, I knew you had it in for me, but I didn't think you'd kill two of your own just to get a chance to torture me to death."

"I didn't kill them so I could kill you myself. I did it to save you."

"Say again?"

"To save you. Because I owe you."

Silfer's look of amazement only deepened. "Owe me? I fucking blackmailed you. You hate me."

The angel sighed, as if preparing to make a great personal confession. "Silfer, that night I spent with you and the succubus sisters was the greatest experience of my entire existence. I know you only set it up so you could film it, but still I'm grateful to you. I've been dreaming of them for years. Perhaps now, with the three worlds colliding, I can finally be with them again."

"Yeah," said Silfer, feeling like a bastard. "Maybe you can be."

"And you? Are you off to see your mortal beloved?"

Silfer nodded.

"Good," said the angel. "I wish you all the best. Love knows no boundaries, Silfer. It is stronger than God and the Devil. It is the only force in this universe that is truly worthy of devotion. Now if I can only get another taste of those sweet succubus cunts..." the angel slipped into a rapture.

Silfer dodged out of the building site, running now towards Mara's apartment.

Frogs splattered under his boots. Untold horrors unfolded before his eyes as abominations from a Bosch fever dream arrived to ravage humanity. A sense of joy swelled within him. *Only one more block!* His heart soared – then sank like a stone as he saw her apartment building engulfed in flames.

Frogs squirmed on the slippery grass. Mara did her best to move around them, not wanting to add their guts to her filth. Maybe she should have asked one of the looters for an umbrella? She thought about heading back over to the museum. She sure as shit couldn't go back to her house; the place had burst into flames and collapsed just before she'd stepped through the door. She was surprised she hadn't been incinerated by the back draft, but the flames had recoiled as if they'd wished to avoid her – her, or Veles.

Mara walked around towards the front of the building. Its sawtooth frame jutted up into the bruised sky. She heard gunfire and trumpets and horrible singing. She saw angels with ripped wings, severed limbs, and warm bloody rain. The apocalypse had been going on for almost three hours at least, but she wasn't even enjoying it. It was meaningless without him. Where was her demon? Where was her love? She and Silfer had talked about almost everything, yet both had failed to mention any sort of meeting place. That was poor planning on her part, she supposed. She cursed herself as she turned the corner –

Then froze, feeling the pull of a smile at the corner of her lips. Oh, there he was. Standing in front of her building, looking forlorn. She should have expected as much; he was always showing up where she least expected him.

Mara came to stand beside him, but he was busy surveying the damage to the house. He seemed more upset about it than she was, and he didn't even live there.

"It's not a big deal," Mara said. "I've got renter's insurance. That'll cover some of it. I pay enough, fucking criminals. Jesus, what happened to your ears?"

Silfer's heart hammered when he heard her voice. He turned to see her standing beside him, smiling in the crimson rain, amongst the ruins of the city. For a moment he was speechless. He dropped his rifle and wrapped his arms around her. Mara rested against him. His grip grew even tighter as he muttered words of love into her hair.

"Hey," she said, patting his arm. "You're squeezing too tight. I can't breathe."

"Sorry," he said, relaxing his grip. He gazed into her eyes, wiping trails of blood and soot from her face. In the background people were screaming, angels were singing, demons were swearing. The entirety of the cosmos was collapsing in on itself. But neither of them cared. Neither looked away from the other.

"Mara," he said. "Mara, I..."

Mara was tired of talking. She smeared her mouth to his. For once they didn't need words.

About the Authors

B.J. SWANN is the incarnation of a demon who shall not be named. Which makes him sort of like Jesus or the Dalai Lama, only not lame. He has come to earth to bring about the Aeon of Chaos, an age of madness, mayhem, and pleasures undreamed of.

www.aeonofchaos.com

ELIZABETH BEDLAM writes whatever the hell she wants from the Black Thorn Care Home in Michigan, about an hour south of Hell. She chases the dragon on Sundays while studying esoteric texts with her dwarf pygmy goat, The Lord of Flies.

www.elizabethbedlam.com

Also By

B.J. Swann

The Crimson Crown

Inverted Dreams. Excoriated Hearts. Terror and Horror Sublime. The twin princesses Oda and Honey are as different as night and day. Oda is a child of the dark, obsessed with cruelty and death. Honey is as sweet as her name, filled with goodwill and compassion. It is therefore a remarkably revolting twist of fate when the royal astrologer orders Oda to be married to the mild-mannered King Armand, while Honey is betrothed to King Barbus of Gutgirt, the most brutal man in the world, who tears peasants apart with his bare hands and keeps his murdered brides' bodies on display in his own bloody chamber.

As the twins strive to wrest back their lives from the cruel hand of fate, they embark on a journey of self discovery that will twist them in unimaginable ways – and perhaps bare the secrets of their innermost selves. At the center of their struggles, shining balefully over all, is the Crimson Crown of Gutgirt, a relic of terrible mystery and demonic power, whose secrets hold the key to salvation – and everlasting doom.

B.J. Swann
Our Lady of the Scythe

"Hogwarts and Camp Halfblood, move the HELL over; there's a new boarding school in town and it is not for the kiddies!" - Christine Morgan, Splatterpunk Award-winning author of Lakehouse Infernal

Eighteen-year-old Raza has a problem: every time she tries to get busy with a boy, she turns into a monster and tears him apart. Why? Because her father is the Big Horned Bastard, demon supreme. To unlock the mysteries of her birthright - and hopefully get some sex education - she's sent to Our Lady of the Scythe, a boarding school for demon-spawn where detention is a realm of flesh-eating monsters and the delinquents get their kicks out of mass murder. Will she even survive the first semester? And what happens when she and her new friends stumble on a vile angelic plot that threatens the survival of all demon kind? Raza will have to embrace her inner demon fast, or kiss her butt goodbye.

Available in Print and Digital from Amazon, and in print only from any good bookstore

B.J. Swann

The Second Wolf

*Bestial Violence. Monstrous Lust.
Total Mayhem.*

A Beast stalks the forests and moors around the city of Stubbe, raping and killing by night, vanishing by day. As the bodies of mangled victims pile up, the citizens grow increasingly terrified – and violent. Unable to stop or trap the elusive Beast, or fathom the cause of its inhuman lusts, the local constabulary is forced to seek help from an outsider in the form of Rubria Caracalla, a beautiful monster hunter of vague but lethal reputation. But Rubria is no ordinary monster hunter, and her perverted plans for the Beast are not the same as those of her patrons.

"The Second Wolf" is a Punk As Fuck fantasy story featuring elements of horror, erotica, and irreverent humour. It contains graphic sex, violence, and potentially disturbing material. It is not intended for children or the easily offended.

Available exclusively from www.god-less.com